The Sasquatch Chronicles

Scott Patterson

ISBN: 979-8-9907112-0-4

PUBLISHED BY: Scott Patterson

The heavens will open to decree the day,
And God shall peer out over the land.
The snow will fall across the dimly lit stone,
And the ground shall weep in sorrow.
The animals will run, and be exposed,
As the machines sputter to a final rest.
And they shall perish,
Like the time that weathers the buildings that succeed them.
The last trees will fall,
And they shall stand alone.
Naked,
And with no place to hide.
The ground will tremble as destruction becomes,
And the heavens shall explode with pity.
And his race,
Like those before him,
Shall be no more.

– Psalm from the Scrolls of the Keepers

I

COMING HOME

I

COMING HOME

The snow swirled, forming a small white tornado, as the sun slowly began to glisten upon the one lone, majestic bald peak. The crisp green pine trees, jetting almost halfway up the peak and covering the somewhat calmer-looking mountains below, now shone a sparkling white. The aspen trees had barely enough time to change, leaving scattered, dense groves of dull reds and gold, trying desperately to peek out from the glittering frost.

He stepped from his small tin mobile home, enjoying the view. He breathed in the cold air and watched as snow blew and danced on top of the bare peak.

The crevices and Y-shaped ravines water had made while making its getaway down the steep cliff for centuries were barely visible, and the deep saddle to the left, which a glacier had left behind almost a million years ago, was beginning to fill with snow and ice.

It had been cold last night, and Jack Frost had been hard at work. It looked like winter was making its appearance early this year. The picturesque postcard beauty seemed as if God himself were trying to say that the celebration of the birth of his son would soon be on its way.

"Merry Christmas indeed," John mumbled, walking down his stairs and heading towards his old red-and-primer-colored truck. Summer seemed so short this year, and winter's fight had already begun. Christmas was just around the corner, and the snow and bitter cold were already here.

What little work he had would start thinning, and the days would become shorter. The snow would fall, and work would be missed. A chill ran down his spine as he thought about being outside in the subzero weather, pounding nails, and praying he could find some inside remodel work.

Two years ago seemed like the right time to start his construction company. News of a ski area had been rumored. The town began to boom, and he had put together enough work to last five years.

Unfortunately, the town quickly overbuilt, he became overextended, and the ski area fell through. Now, he was left hustling any job he could find, trying to hold back his creditors and stay alive. Money had been challenging in the past, but never like this. It was hard enough to pay his one employee, but keeping enough for his personal bills and being able to buy groceries was nearly impossible. His phone continuously rang with bill collectors, and now he was being reminded that it was almost that festive time of the year again.

He had enough work to keep his lenders at arm's length, but the economy was in a slump, interest rates were rising, and the housing market wasn't what it was in the past. He had developed a relationship with his creditors through hours of negotiations, but no matter how they tried to work with him, it never left him with enough to cover much else.

He had no idea how he would get the money to buy presents for his kids and couldn't imagine their faces on Christmas morning with nothing under the tree. The only prayer he had this year was to kill a deer during hunting season. Then, he could take the grocery money and spend it on gifts instead.

He pulled open the door of his old pickup and climbed in, popping the key into the ignition and twisting it to the side while pumping the gas pedal. The old motor whirred and then went silent. He laid his head on the top of his hands, breathed in, and slowly exhaled a foggy mist. He pumped the pedal again, grabbed the keys, and twisted. *Click*. He lifted his head, looking through the foggy window at a large ice-covered car. He smiled, opened his door, and slid from the truck, trudging towards it.

He slapped the Cadillac emblem on the hood and started down the side of the "boat on wheels." He pushed the button on the door handle. It creaked as the door slowly opened. *It's not that bad of a car*, he thought as he climbed in, slamming the door.

The left corner panel had been crushed, and there were some areas where the paint had begun to chip, but he had it running like a top, the electric windows and seats worked, and most importantly, it still had that Cadillac emblem on the hood.

He had dreamed about owning a Cadillac since he was a child, and even though this was the same year and model he had fantasized about, the ones in his fantasies were always a little newer and shinier.

A friend of his was financially in a bad way and had to let it go for seven hundred dollars. Knowing how desperately his friend needed the money, he talked him down to five hundred and made him fill it with gas to *finalize the deal*.

"Yeah, it was a real steal," he laughed as his hot breath iced up the windshield, and a shiver suddenly jumped down his spine. He jerked his head to the side, popping the bones inside while searching for the key ring in his hand. He grabbed the ignition key, glanced at his house, and watched as his cold, calloused hand inserted the key into the ignition.

The hammers and saws had been rough on him over the years, and his five-foot-eight-inch frame wouldn't last forever. He felt stronger than ever, but the years of heavy lifting had started to take its toll, and he could feel it aching down to his bones.

He started his business to get the hammer out of his hand and some decent money in his pocket. But with the economy being what it was and the cash flow so sporadic, he had been taking care of everything. The bidding, buying, building, and bookkeeping.

One other man helped with the building, but he was just a kid with other things on his mind. He fantasized about his company becoming successful so he wouldn't be the one pounding the nails anymore, and he quickly realized that if things didn't get better soon, he would be the one looking for another job.

Another job, he thought. He hated the idea of working for someone else and showed it by rebelling against them. He hadn't had any schooling as far as college was concerned, and that's what he believed it took to get the "good jobs" that paid well, had good benefits, and treated you like a real person. The "good jobs" that always seemed to elude him.

College was never an option for him. The Army was. When he was nineteen, his wife was pregnant with his son, and he had to do the *right* thing. Joining the Army was the only way he knew of paying the medical bills, and he spent four years in hell for it. The only other training he had, besides the skill he now possessed, was a dream that died long ago.

Words of prodigy once circled his home after his mother bought an old, beat-up piano at a garage sale. He started picking at it, fixed it up, and somehow got it tuned. He spent all his spare time playing and studying it. He loved that piano more than anything.

His father, however, hated it and sold it soon after he noticed John's intense interest and realized how much it could be sold for. He chastised John for thinking about playing and tried

12

desperately to beat the thoughts of music out of him. His father never allowed another instrument in the house.

Sometime later, his mother surprised him by sneaking in a small electronic keyboard and a pair of headphones she bought by working through her lunch hours. She worked long hours at the same retail store for as long as he could remember, and her overtime pay went unnoticed by his father.

When she could, she would cash her checks before coming home and set aside a little money. It could have gone to many other places, but she always seemed to pull through when it came to matters of her heart. It was their secret that had been kept to this day.

The car slowly whined and went silent. He turned off the key, pumped the gas, and flicked it back on. "Damn it," he heaved as the engine clicked, and he lay his head on the steering wheel. It was colder last night than he thought. He grabbed the door handle, slapping the top of the dashboard with two fingers out of frustration.

The vinyl cracked, spreading towards the windshield, stopping just before it reached the glass. John stared in disbelief, smacked his palm against the steering wheel, and stepped from the car. He slammed the door behind him, stomping towards his home.

The dull brown paint on the tin siding was chipping, exposing the original green underneath, and the skirting he made with leftover wood from various jobs he had worked was starting to rot. The stairs, made from the same fashion, were beginning to loosen, and he noticed that the roof was starting to bow.

He thought about the dream house he had built in his mind a thousand times and wondered where he had gone wrong in life. He wiggled the stairs and looked back at the blowing snow on the peak. *There was something there,* he thought, as he grabbed the knob and pushed open the door.

He stepped into his living room and looked at his watch. It was Six-thirty. It was a good thing he couldn't sleep and got up early. He would call Phil around seven and ask him to come over and jump his truck. They could leave from here and still be on the job in plenty of time. It was already coming in late, and another hour wouldn't make a difference one way or the other.

He glanced through the room, subconsciously taking inventory. The old ranch-style couch and chair, coffee table, wood-burning stove, television, and large bookshelf that divided the kitchen and living room was about all this room could hold. He looked into the kitchen and stopped abruptly at an empty champagne and vodka bottle on the counter.

He shivered, threw his coat on the chair, and walked towards the small wood-burning stove. He sighed and squatted, opening the doors and looking inside. The fire he tried to make before going outside hadn't taken. He grabbed the logs inside, pulling them out. He crumpled some newspapers into a ball, shoved them through the cavity the doors provided, and blew on the ash. He placed the logs he pulled out onto the burning paper and stared at the flame. Satisfied it would start, he stood, closed the doors, and twisted the handles to secure them.

He walked to the kitchen, grabbed the empty bottles, and threw them in the trash. He looked around momentarily and grabbed a coffee cup from the cupboard. He poured coffee from the pot he had made earlier into it, lit a cigarette, and walked down the hall past the small bathroom.

He stepped into his bedroom, smelling the remnants of the alcohol his wife had drunk the night before. The end of his cigarette glowed red as he inhaled and exhaled a cloud of smoke while looking at her.

14

She lay quietly in an oversized bed that left just enough room to squeeze in a small dresser and allowing a narrow path to the closet. She always liked the finer things in life, and a king-sized water bed was one she couldn't live without. Her head popped out from under the blankets, and she ran her fingers through her hair, pulling it back and exposing her face.

He looked into her eyes, remembering why he had fallen in love with her, and smiled. She twisted her head around, slammed it into the pillow, and huffed, closing her eyes. She was a small woman, only reaching John's chest, and it didn't look like she had gained an ounce of weight since they met. Her facial features reminded him of an angel, and her eyes shone a crystal blue.

He wondered how she kept herself so beautiful through these strenuous years and sighed, knowing she would stay beautiful forever. He had fallen in love with her as a teenager and found his love, together with her beauty, growing more every day. It was often the only strength he had to pull himself through. But now, even that started to become blurry.

She started drinking soon after Kirsten was born, and his father's personality began reflecting in her almost immediately. He began noticing the bags and wrinkles around her eyes, and just as quickly, her beauty started fading along with his love.

"Hey," he spoke softly, waiting for a reply and placing his hand on her waist. "Hey." Her eyes opened, staring at him, and closed. "Hey." He quietly spoke again.

"What?!" she replied, irritated and drowsy.

"Don't you think it's about time for you to be getting up?"

"Are Zach and Kirsten up?"

"No."

15

"Then don't worry about it for a while." She threw the blanket over her head and rolled onto her stomach, attempting to go back to sleep.

He gulped down the last of his coffee and looked at her. The end of his cigarette turned a bright red and subsided. He didn't know what had gone wrong, but he knew he didn't want to live like this much longer. He stood, still looking at her, then walked to the kitchen to refill his empty cup. He sighed and walked through the hall into his children's room.

His son, Zach, lay in the top bunk while his daughter, Kirsten, lay in the bottom with her covers kicked off. He glanced at the dresser on the back wall and then back to the bed filling the tiny room. *They deserve so much better than this*, he thought, taking another drink and sighing again. Except for the crayon marks along the bottom of the wall and the absence of beer cans on the floor, it looked like a scaled-down version of a friend's college dorm room he visited when he was still in high school.

Zach moaned, rolling over. John paused, standing still while trying to be quiet. He wondered what Zach's life would be like as he moved closer to the other bed in the room. He kneeled down, looking at his little girl peacefully sleeping. He pulled the covers over her petite body and kissed her on the forehead, whispering, "Your daddy loves you," in her ear.

He would never be able to forgive himself if they had to go through life like he did.

He put the cigarette to his mouth, gently sucking the end of it, and removed it, blowing only clean air. He looked at the burned-out butt and placed it between his thumb and forefinger, pressing and compacting it. He looked at his son's face as he tucked blankets around him, still holding the butt in his hand.

16

The stove crackled in the background. He forgot to close the vents. He hurried into the hot living room. He turned the handle on the chimney pipe above, and smoke escaped through the slots in the air valve below. He bent down, screwing the air valve on tight, looked at the cigarette butt still in his hand, opened one of the doors, and tossed it in.

Tiny beads of sweat covered his forehead as he stood. He wiped the sweat from his head and stood. The twelve-by-sixty-foot trailer looked awfully small and felt even smaller. He wiped his hands on his pants, thinking again about how living in his dream home would feel. He breathed in, guzzling the rest of his coffee, and walked into the kitchen.

"What are you doing up so early?" Sheila whispered as she appeared from the hall.

"I don't know. Just couldn't sleep, I guess."

"God, do you think it's hot enough in here?" She waved her hand in front of her face while walking to the refrigerator and opened the door. "Are you hungry?"

"Yeah, I guess." He poured himself another cup of coffee and set it on the kitchen table, sitting in the chair next to it.

She clanged a pan as she pulled it from the bottom cabinet and placed it on the stove. "Is there something wrong with the truck?"

"Dead battery, I think." He shook from the caffeine he had been ingesting all morning, trying not to show his irritation at the noise she was making. He took another drink of his coffee, setting down his cup.

"And the Caddy?"

"Same thing. You know, if I had known that it was going to get this cold, I would've plugged the charger in. But I didn't, so let's just drop it, okay?"

17

The silence became deafening as she peeled the bacon from the package and slapped it into the pan. "Is Phil coming over?"

"I was going to call him around seven. Will you please just let me worry about my own life?" He stood and walked toward the counter. "I think I can handle it." He grabbed the bread from the drawer and tossed a couple of pieces into the toaster, shoving down on the dispenser.

"Now, wait a minute, buddy. Just because you've had a bad morning doesn't mean you have to take it out on me."

He looked at her, grabbed the fresh pot of coffee she had made, and walked to the kitchen table, filling his cup. He placed the pot back in the maker and took a large drink as he sat at the table.

He stared out the window above the sink as the coffee burned the inside of his mouth and throat while making its way to his stomach. He jumped to the freezer, grabbed a piece of ice, and tossed it in his mouth. He crunched it, trying to stop the burning without being obvious about it as he sat down.

"Will you be here when the kids get up?" she asked, setting down a plate of bacon and eggs before him.

"I don't know, Sheila, it all depends on what time Phil gets here," he said, touching the new blisters in his mouth with his tongue.

Kirsten stumbled into the kitchen, rubbing her eyes. She was almost two and had the same features as her mother. Her blonde hair ran straight down the middle of her little back in what seemed like the same braid forever, and her sky-blue eyes popped out from under her hands. She reached out her arms. "Mommy," she whined, racing towards her mother and standing before her crying.

Sheila bent over, lifted her into her arms, and slowly rocked her back and forth. "What's the matter, honey? Do you have to go potty?"

The baby nodded yes while saying no, and her bottom lip quivered as she breathed in. The crying started again as they disappeared down the hallway and into the bathroom.

John put the last piece of bacon in his mouth, chewing tenderly as Zach entered the room. "Hey, Dad," he muttered as he walked by.

"Hey, Zach," he moaned.

"Just gonna get something to eat." Zach smiled, walking towards the refrigerator and breaking into a ninja fight with an invisible opponent. He threw himself to the ground, laughing hysterically.

It looks like another day in paradise, John thought, blowing on his coffee, ensuring it cooled down. "Get up here and settle down, Zach," he demanded. "You know we don't allow that kind of roughhousing in here."

Zach rolled over, looking at his father and settling down after seeing he was in no mood to play. His olive-colored skin probably led to the same dark eyes and hair as his father's. His stocky eight-year-old body had already begun filling out, and his baby teeth were quickly being pushed away, leaving small gaps in the front of his mouth. John gazed at him and hoped, as he always did, that he would be able to do the things for them that were never done for him.

Sheila walked into the kitchen, still carrying Kirsten, and looked at Zach, who was lying on the floor.

"Hi, Mom, what's for breakfast?"

"It's in the pan, Zach. Now go wash your hands, and I'll have it ready for you when you're done."

Zach jumped from the ground, flying to the bathroom, imitating an airplane as he went. Sheila sat on the chair, still trying to quiet Kirsten and looking at John. "Do you think you could give me a little help?"

"Sure," he said, standing and walking to the stove. He reheated the breakfast she had made earlier and looked at a magnetic plaque hanging on the hood above him. "To live fully is to live freely..." She loved hanging these little sayings around the house. They made it look more "*homey*," she would always say. "...To take each day and make it all your own..."

Zach zipped out of the bathroom, attacking his father's leg.

"Whoa, wait a minute, Zach," John yelled, surprised by the sudden jolt. "It's almost ready, so go sit down so you can eat."

He grabbed the pan and looked back at the sign as Zach ran to the table. Zach slammed into the chair, sending John's coffee mug flying to the floor. No wonder it was left anonymous, he thought, grabbing a dishtowel from under the sink, throwing it over the spill.

He looked at Zach and Kirsten as he put food on their plates and thought about the days that each were born. Zach was a complete surprise and almost didn't make it. He wasn't breathing when he came out. John stood in shock as they moved his blue body to a table, removing the umbilical cord from around his neck. After what seemed like forever, he started crying, and they put him in John's arms, quickly taking him back and carrying him from the room.

He and Sheila had to stay in the hospital for a couple of days. He had never felt love like he did that night. He had a son, and it was the best day of his life. A few years later, Sheila decided if they had one, they might as well have two, and she was soon pregnant again.

He put the pans into the sink and drank the rest of his coffee, looking at the three of them sitting around the table.

They almost didn't make it to the hospital with Kirsten. By the time he dropped Sheila off at the emergency entrance, parked the car, and ran inside, Kirsten was already lying on the bed. The nurse

20

put her in his arms, commenting about how he must be the father, and scuttled him towards the nursery.

She looked like an elf, and he thought she was the ugliest baby he had ever seen. He rubbed his nose on hers, welcoming her into the world as he carried her towards the nursery. He felt even more love than he had with Zach. All he wanted was to protect her. It was absolutely the best day he'd ever had.

He set down his cup, walked to the living room, and plopped into the chair, picking up the phone. He dialed Phil's number and sighed as Phil answered. "Hello Phil, I've run into a problem over here...

I-II

The soft, cool snow felt good on the pads of Roa-Ma's feet as he ran along the top of a mountain range he had been following for the past two days. He was behind schedule and had time to make up. His family would expect him soon, and he didn't like the idea of them looking for him.

He entered a small clearing, staring at a single white peak sparkling in the light of the nearly full moon in the distance. He looked at the trees around him and then at the valley below. He stopped, staring at the distant, barely visible miles of white-capped peaks to the West, which disappeared from view on both sides.

His eyes followed the trees encircling the field before him and stopped at animal tracks entering or exiting the barren area. He lifted his nose in the air, breathing deeply, then navigated his way through the forest to investigate.

He looked at the string of white peaks again, kneeling down and feeling the disturbed snow that surrounded the prints the animal had left behind. He stood, scanning the area around him, breathing silently and listening intently as his eyes followed the prints through the snow.

He picked up a piece of the animal's excrement from a pile lying in the series of tracks and squeezed it between his thumb and forefinger, forming a tight ball while bringing it to his nose, sniffing it, and flicking it to the ground.

It was a single elk that had been here the night before. He stood looking at the mountain before him and gazed back at the glistening peaks in the distance. He exhaled a cloud of misty smoke, looked at the elk's tracks, and breathed deeply. He exhaled, starting on his path toward the summit of the peak that lay ahead.

It snowed through the night, and the moisture in the air had left a slight covering of snow and ice over everything in sight. With the bright moon shining, the thought of crossing this peak without any protection from the trees made him nervous. He debated waiting an extra day before crossing, but knew time was running short. He looked at the sky above him and ran faster, knowing he would be lucky to make it before the break of day.

A light reflected ahead of him, and he quickly became part of the nearest tree, standing motionless. He squatted, carefully moving his head from behind the tree and jerking it back. He sat, holding his breath, hearing nothing. A brownish-white rabbit with a cotton tail darted behind him. He twisted his body, reached for it, lost his balance, and slammed onto his back.

He snapped his head towards the light with his heart beating wildly, and his breath becoming short. Nothing. He breathed out, relieved, and leaned forward, pulling himself up. The light reappeared. He snapped back to the ground, and it disappeared. He looked at the moon, slowly stood, and shook his head, as he cautiously started towards the reflection in the snow.

He reached two metal beams, causing the glare, and turned his head from one side to the other, watching as the antique narrow-gauge railroad tracks faded from view. A stream trickled in the background, and a bird took flight. Instantly, he was back in the trees, lifting his nose high and breathing deeply, trying to detect a scent. He stood silent for a moment and continued on his journey without a sound.

The branches and ice snapped under his feet as the small path he found crumbled, sending dirt and rocks down the steep incline. It was the earliest and hardest start of winter he could remember. The herds of deer and elk would be forced to lower grounds earlier this year in search of food, and hunting season would quickly approach. The guns would start exploding, and many of them would die.

The moon slowly disappeared behind a cloud, and he hastened his pace. The packed snow and ice steadily grew deeper and popped under his massive weight every few steps he took. His adrenaline raced as he stumbled deeper into the snow with the sound of the breaking ice reverberating through the mountains, like the gunshots in the valleys that echoed through his mind.

Dead and dwarfed trees, showing scars of lightning strikes, dotted the forest and became more frequent as he approached an altitude where they could no longer live. He slowed his pace and cautiously stepped forward, stopping at the edge of a large boulder. He looked at the top of the bald peak and then into the increasingly lighter gray sky. He looked at the now-visible peaks to the West and then at the barren plains that extended eastward.

The beauty here always took his breath, and he loved stopping, but he wasn't even close to the summit, and the sun would be coming up soon. There was nowhere for him to hide. His timing wasn't as good as it used to be, and he would be taking a chance of being seen.

He looked upon the vast wilderness of trees and lights from the cities and towns below, and then at the mountains containing his destination. It was amazing how little time it took for these towns to multiply and move ever closer to his home. He blinked at the sea of white before him and hid next to another boulder springing from the ground.

He hated this part and knew he was on dangerous ground. Making this crossing with the first rays of the sun wasn't making him feel better, and he wondered how he timed this so poorly. His fist pounded through the icy crust and grabbed the virgin snow below. He squeezed it in his hand and leaned back on the rock, sucking the water it held.

A loud explosion boomed, breaking the silence. He moved his head around the rock, scanning the ocean-like white above him, and pointed his nose towards the sky, inhaling the air. A bird landed on the rock above him, singing to the breaking day. He twisted his neck, glaring at the bird, and threw the ice ball in his mouth. He squatted further behind the boulder, still searching the open crest, and smelled for some kind of scent.

The reverberation occurred again, rumbling through the mountains. He looked at a small rocky crag hiding on the edge of the peak and squinted his eyes, trying to find where the sound originated. He angled up the steep terrain, trying to view the rock formation, and reached the peak's highest point. He sat on the cold ice and snow, and the crags fully appeared. A shiver ran up his spine, and he became motionless, staring at the rocks in the distance.

The sun started crawling up the back of the mountain range, blazing over the top of the peak, and a gust of wind swirled snow around and above him. He squinted, becoming snow-blind, and the ground gleamed in blues, reds, and crystal-like whites. He snapped his neck to the side, popping the vertebrae inside, and the mountain shook again. He squinted his eyes tighter, trying to block the glare, and caught the movement of a grayish-white figure on one of the crags below.

He zigzagged down the steep, barren terrain, affording himself a better view, and half sat, half stood on a ledge, bracing himself against the mountain, clutching the earth with his massive claws. A small herd of big horn sheep were in search of food, while two young males butted heads on the rocks above. His eyes widened with compassion and relief as he relaxed, his smile broadening at the sight below.

The wind died and suddenly gusted again, jolting the front of him. He lay back from the force and closed his eyes as the ice underneath him gave way with a loud crack, sending sharp rocks into his back. The sheep froze, scanning the area where he sat.

The males' breath misted as they stuck their noses in the air, smelling for danger, and the ewes watched poignantly. The rams looked at each other and, not sensing any danger, stood on their hind legs, charging one another again.

The ewes watched them resume their play and simultaneously dropped their heads, kicking their hooves at the ice, in search of the elusive food below. The ram's horns met, snapping like two large sticks forcibly striking each other, sending an echo through the valley and knocking them both backward.

He turned his attention to a large city in the east and a smaller town to the North. He wondered how the valleys must have looked before they built the cities and how his ancestors could roam freely throughout the land without fear. He lifted a strap off his shoulder and over his head. He grabbed a leather pouch hanging almost to his waist, dug his hand inside, and pulled out some of the seeds, cactus tops, and berries he had collected from the lower grounds the day before.

He popped the berries and cactus tops into his mouth, sprinkled some seeds into the gusting wind, and carefully folded the flap back over the top. He dropped the bag over his neck and breathed a tired sigh as the wind suddenly died. His hot breath turned the biting cold to a fine white, misty fog rising above his head.

He still had a long way to go, and home sounded better now than at any other time he could remember. The wind gusted again, forcing him back onto the ice and sharp rocks. He lowered his arms to his waist, pulled himself up, and instantly, he was back on the path that led him home.

I-III

A dark sports car pulled close to the small trailer and stopped, honking the horn. "Phil's here," Sheila yelled, clearing the table and looking out the small window above the sink. She walked towards it, looked at Phil's car, and placed the dishes under the faucet.

"All right, tell him I'll be there in a minute," John yelled, looking in the mirror and pulling at his face, searching for blackheads. He paused, squeezed a few select places, stepped over to the toilet, and sighed as the coffee he had been drinking continued to run through him.

Sheila walked to the door, stuck her head outside, and waved her finger in the air. Phil smiled, waving back and acknowledging her as he turned down his radio. She waved again, pulling back the hair blowing on her face, and closed the door, walking to the table.

She picked up her coffee cup, listening to her husband in the bathroom and the children playing in their bedroom. She stepped to the cupboard, pulled down a small bottle of vodka, splashed some of the liquid in her cup, and quickly placed it back on the shelf, quietly closing the door.

John bolted from the bathroom, still pulling at his zipper. He ran through the kitchen and to the living room as Sheila nervously turned and walked to the table, setting down her cup. He grabbed his coat from the coat rack and walked towards his wife. "We've got a lot of work to do, and the job was supposed to be done yesterday, so I'll probably be late. Okay?"

She looked through her cup, picked it up, and glanced in his eyes. "You know, John, it is Friday, and I was thinking that it might be a good idea if we went out tonight." She smiled, glancing back at her cup, as he watched her silently. "You know," she looked at him again, "To help take some of the stress away? You've been working awfully hard lately, and I think you deserve it. Don't you?"

And where am I supposed to get the money for this? Flashed through his mind as she took a drink from her cup, and he could smell alcohol. "I know. We'll see when I get home, okay?" She tried to smile, achieving a sad, desperate look instead, and swallowed more of her drink. "Listen, it'll be late when I get home, so if we don't make it tonight, I promise we'll go this weekend, okay?" He kissed her on the cheek, and she nodded her head, knowing he meant they weren't going anywhere tonight or any other night.

He hurried towards the kids' room and watched as Zach was busy getting ready for school. Kirsten followed him around, imitating his every move. "Hey, Zach," he said, "come here for a minute."

Kirsten followed as Zach exhaled in disapproval and approached his father. The little girl nudged her way closer, putting herself between her brother and her father as John dropped to one knee, pulling her close to his chest. He unbuttoned Zach's crooked shirt and began re-buttoning it correctly.

"If she'd leave me alone, I could do it myself, Dad. Can't you get her to leave me alone?"

"Look, Daddy, mine needs buttoned too," Kirsten happily stated while stepping back from John's chest, showing him her zipper.

"I see that," John smiled, "but first, you need some buttons." He ran his fingers down the front of her blanket sleeper, making her laugh, and straightened his son's collar. He ensured his son appeared presentable, and Kirsten worked her way onto his knee. He held her

29

steady, touching his son's side. "Now I've got to go to work, Zach. I'll give Kirsten to your mother, but you make sure you be at school on time. You hear?"

"Yes, sir," Zach mumbled, nodding his head.

"All right then." He smiled, standing and heaving his daughter into his arms. He looked at Zach and stroked his hair. He held Kirsten tight and bent down, softly kissing the top of his head. "Have a good day, son, okay?"

"I will," Zach said, looking at his father, still nodding his head, tucking in his shirt, and buttoning his pants.

"I know you will. You're a good kid." He held Zach's jaw in his hand, running his fingers up and down his cheek, sighed, and walked out the door, closing it behind him. Zach ran to his bed, slipped on his socks and shoes, listened at the door for his father to leave, and swung it open, rushing to the living room.

The clean, fresh air filled John's lungs as he stood on his stairs, inhaling deeply. The hot sun warmed his face; the stairs wiggled beneath him, and his eyes tried to adjust to the blinding white snow. Phil's shadowy torso climbed from the car, leaning on the open door and roof. "So, what's the plan, boss?"

"Just pull it over to the truck, and we'll jump it!" he yelled, digging the sunglasses from his top pocket and placing them over his eyes.

Phil jumped behind the wheel of his car, pulled it in front of the truck, and pulled the lever under the dash, popping the hood. As John approached, he got out and sat on the front side panel. John reached the back of his truck, grabbed the jumper cables lying in the bed, and threw them at his employee. He opened the truck door and yanked the lever under his dashboard.

Phil caught the cables and jumped off his car, trying not to look at his boss, who was getting closer. He was an attractive young man

30

with dark brown eyes, a baseball cap that covered his brown hair, and a height that towered above John. His lean body still hadn't filled out, and a diamond-studded earring sparkled from his left ear.

Phil lifted the truck's hood, exposing the engine and battery. He turned to his car and placed his hand under the hood, tugging on the latch and pulling it up. He squeezed the clips on the ends of the cables, connecting them to the metal studs on his car's battery, while holding the other two clips in his hand and being careful not to touch them to any metal or to each other.

"I didn't wake up your mom and dad this morning, did I?" John asked as he stood watching Phil connect the cables to the truck's battery. John resented Phil for being twenty-two years old and still living at home with his parents. He resented even more that they would pay his bills and buy him the car he was driving. He had been paying his own way since his father sold his piano and found him a job. It was his way of occupying his time and teaching him the *"responsibilities of life."*

Now, he couldn't imagine what life would be like without responsibilities, and sometimes it seemed that just looking at Phil reminded him of how heavy his load was. Phil turned around and looked at him with a smile as he lifted his sunglasses and placed them on his forehead. "Oh, I wouldn't worry about it."

"What happened to you?" John blurted out, stunned. He walked towards his employee, touching the bruised area under his eye.

"Come on, man, it still hurts." Phil winced, lifting his arm and slapping John's hand from his face.

"Were you at the Steer last night?" He grinned, finding the mark under Phil's eye humorous.

"Where else is there?" Phil answered, gazing toward the white peak before them.

31

"Was it Bobby? It was Bobby, wasn't it?"

"I'm not feelin' real good, John. Let me get some sleep, and I'll tell you all about it later, okay?"

"What's the matter, bud, hungover?" He laughed in his face. "Too much to drink, and then Bobby Cantrell whoops your ass." He laughed harder. "Boy, I wish I could have been there to see that." He walked to the door of his truck, trying to keep a straight face, and snickered into a full laugh as he pulled it open. "I told you you shouldn't be messin' with his old lady." He pointed his head to the sky, cackling, and climbed into his car.

Phil coldly watched John close the door and mumble obscenities while he waited to pull off the cables and move his car. John knocked on the inside of his truck's windshield, capturing Phil's attention. He pointed at him while laughing and twisted the key. The truck backfired, blowing out black smoke, and began coldly running.

The truck bounced as John threw it in third gear. He grabbed the steering wheel with both hands and pulled it back on course, navigating it down the pothole-filled dirt street. Phil crouched in the seat, catching his balance, and readjusted his position. He tipped the cap off his eyes and looked at John. "Isn't it about time for you to step up to a real car?"

John pulled a cigarette from his pocket, tapped it on the top of his steering wheel, and looked at Phil as he placed the butt in his mouth. "Well, Phil, anytime your daddy wants to dump another thirty-five grand," he started, digging in his pocket for his lighter. "I'd be glad to step right on up."

Phil was a natural carpenter. His artistic abilities and understanding of angles made him a quick study, and with his situation being what it was, he was willing to work cheap. John

32

trusted him completely behind a saw, but thought he needed to learn some boundaries and have the chip knocked from his shoulder.

Phil slipped his hat back over his eyes. "Well, I think you keep it around to remind you of your Army days," he mumbled, not meaning to be heard.

"And just what in the hell is that supposed to mean?"

"Nothing, man. Just leave me alone and let me get some sleep, will ya?"

"Now, you let me tell you something, man. I served this country so that you could live your way of life. I didn't have any other choices, man, and anytime somebody wants to give me one, I'd be glad to take it." He leaned back, slamming the steering wheel with his hand and turning red in the face.

I-IV

The snow silently dissipated, turning to mud as the sun beat down, warming the earth and melting the ice covering the higher peaks and mountains. Roa-Ma continued dropping in elevation as the trees became more abundant and the forest thickened. The soft ground below his feet padded his steps, loosening his back and allowing him more speed.

A small squirrel scampered onto the trail ahead of him and froze, staring at the large object quickly approaching. Roa-Ma sped his pace, and the squirrel darted from the trail, climbing a large tree. He slowed, watching it jump from the branch of one tree to the branch of another, disappearing into the forest and chirping on its way. He picked up his pace to a gallop and quickly continued through the forest like an animal pursuing its prey.

His arms hung at his side, swinging back and forth in the time of a metronome as twigs, branches, and dead leaves crushed under his massive weight. The mountain range broke up ahead and opened into a valley below. It was time to head west, going over the mountains instead of following this range.

He decelerated his speed, stopping before reaching the edge of the trees, and scanned the valley below. Car windshields flashed from a road in the distance. He slid behind a tree, kneeling next to it, to hide, and slowly stood.

He peeked around the tree, and they flashed again, verifying that they posed no danger. He stepped from behind the branches into the open field, inspecting his surroundings. He became confused, as nothing looked familiar, and looked again at the edge of the mountain, indecisively following it back to the trees.

He lingered in the forest, running at a slight angle towards the edge of the mountain, as a familiar trail approached and passed. He circled around, feeling more confident of his surroundings, and found the trail he had passed. He began running on it with renewed confidence, jumping as the edge of the range appeared before him.

The world seemed to stop as he looked at the ground below and the rocky cliff behind. His eyes grew wide with fear, and the wind gushed through his hair as the ground hurled closer, threatening to break his fall.

His knees buckled under the strain of his weight, the air left his lungs, and his feet dug forward, covering his legs with dirt as he hit the ground. He fell to his butt, rolled to his side, and was out of control, tumbling and skidding down the steep terrain.

He became wild with panic as his environment streaked by and he searched for a way to stop. He grabbed a large bush protruding from the earth, and its roots snapped with a hollow plunk, tearing out of the dirt and becoming limp in his hand.

A low, animal-like grumble bellowed from his throat as he frantically grabbed onto anything his hands could reach. Rocks and dirt followed him down the incline as large clumps of dying weeds and grass ripped from the mountain. He bounced, looking at the bottom of the hill, furiously trying to reposition his body. The trees rooted in the earth at the bottom of this rocky field were coming fast, and avoiding them would be impossible.

He stretched, grabbing at a small tree approaching on his right. He touched it with his hand, holding it tight. *R-I-I-I-P-P.* He was violently thrown in the air as he rolled onto his belly, clawing at the mountainside. He screamed as his body twisted, and a tree flashed in his eyes. A thunk followed by a snap reverberated through his brain. His body went limp, and everything became black.

He woke with the sun sparkling above him and a narrow stream of water trickling through his hand. He looked at the side of the mountainous cliff he had fallen from and sat up painfully. His body ached, and a sharp pain throbbed through his shoulder and chest. He hung his left arm limply by his side, afraid to move it, and sighed. He looked at the water running through his hand during the night and then back at the cliff.

A small red fox crossed the tree line above him, disappearing behind the rocks. He cupped his right hand, pulled water to his mouth, and wondered where it might be going. He was sure he had found the right path on top of that range, but now he had to face the fact that he was hurt and lost.

He closed his eyes, still dizzy from the fall, and tilted his head, breathing deeply and pointing his nose in the air. The pain sharpened, shooting through his side, and he whimpered, instinctively reaching for it. He screamed, holding his breath and trying to stop the sound from reaching his vocal cords. He pulled his hand away as the pain became unbearable and slowly subsided.

He scanned his surroundings, straightened his body, and meticulously checked his back and upper body with his right hand while bypassing his shoulder and neck. His muscles were tight and sore, but the bones seemed undamaged. He exhaled slowly, moving his hand between his shoulder and neck to apply pressure. He pulled it back to his side, breathing in and holding his breath as the sting painfully throbbed, working its way through his body.

His arm hung motionless as he looked through the cliff ahead, hoping it was a fracture that wouldn't need to be set. His hand glided over his hips and down his thighs as he bent his legs, checking his calves, shins, and feet. He had no idea where he was and prayed that a large river ran somewhere in the valley below. He leaned against the tree he had hit, bracing his back and trying to stand.

The animals scattered, and the birds took flight as the tree echoed a thunderous crack. He hit the ground, crouching in fear and waiting for the tree to make its final blow. It wiggled for a moment and slowly stopped. He lifted his head, still squinting his eyes, and released his breath. He rolled to the ground, lying on his back as his shoulder burned as if a hot knife were intruding on the tendons and bones inside.

He sat for a moment, thinking of his younger years and all the times he had made this journey. *Where could he have gone wrong?* In years past, he could have handled that jump easily. And a falling tree? When he was younger, he could have jumped up and grabbed it before it broke. It wouldn't have mattered if he was hurt or not. He thought of his father's degenerative state during his last days on this land and wondered if he was suffering the same fate.

The wind gusted, shaking the tree and reminding him of the time he lost. He scooted next to it for a closer examination, slowly rubbing his finger up and down the hairline crack that originated about four feet from the bottom. He knew it might take a while to fall, but it would fall. And when it did, it would kill anything that happened to be running by at the time. He waited as the pain subsided and inched his way toward a more structurally sound tree a few feet away.

He sat against it, grabbing the thick branch overhead and pulling himself up. He held his breath, and his face twisted with pain as it tingled through his fingers and hips. He wheezed, anchoring his weight on his rubbery legs, and leaned against the tree, supporting his weight.

He held his hurt arm by his chest and tilted his head towards the sky. He breathed out as the pain lessened, and he lifted his unhurt arm, slowly running his fingers along his shoulder. He pressed on his collarbone, and blood oozed down his chest as the bone pierced the skin. He jerked his hand away, staring in a daze at the passing clouds and slowly swinging his head from side to side. *I don't have time for this*, he thought, wanting to wait before he tried to set the broken bone.

He scanned the area, rubbed his blood between his fingers, and pushed his leather satchel towards his stomach. He unfolded it, grabbed a handful of five-pointed leaves, and laid them on his tongue. His tongue moved them to his cheek, and he bit down, sucking the juices they provided.

He stepped towards the cracked tree, lifted his leg, and angrily kicked it above the break. It popped, and the crack splintered. The tree fell to the ground with a thud. He dropped to his knees as the pain returned, and he wished he had left it to fall on its own. He scanned the area for predators and silently persisted down the steep incline, frustrated by his own incompetence.

The ground leveled as the pain throbbed, and his eyelids partially closed. The pain-killing effect of the leaves had begun. He darted through a small grove of leafless aspen trees, following the sound of running water. *I've got to figure out where I am*, he thought as he re-situated the arm on his chest, holding it tight and picking up his pace.

He screeched to a halt as a large boulder in the shape of a face loomed in front of him. He followed a line of small pine trees standing in perfect line on both sides of it, studying them as he passed. He paused for a moment, thinking of a story he had heard as

38

a child about a gateway identical to this one, leading to a magical place where all things lived in peace and harmony.

A breeze blew on his face, and his heart began pounding. A cold sweat broke on the back of his neck, and he froze, sensing a presence watching him. He slowly turned and flinched, surprised by a small crow sitting on the last tree in the line. It looked over at him and screeched. "Caw, caw!"

He released his arm, hanging it at his side, and leaned against the boulder, exhaling a relieved sigh. "Caw, Caw," he echoed back, smiling. He opened the satchel around his neck and pulled out a handful of seeds, offering them to the bird. The bird took flight, gliding towards him, as he closed his hand around the seeds, holding his good arm high in the air. He dropped it to his chest as the bird landed on his forearm, fluttering its wings and looking him in the eye before becoming still.

"What are you doing? Trying to scare me to death?" He grunted with pain as he opened his hand, exposing the seeds. The crow jerked, looking at the seeds and then back at him. It jerked again, looked at his hand, and pecked the treat it held. It looked at him and lifted its beak into the air, swallowing.

He watched as it continued pecking at his hand and swallowing. The pain became more than he could bear, and he agonizingly looped his arm into the air, scattering the seeds and exciting the bird. He watched it extend its wings, disappearing into the slowly darkening sky.

He walked past the tall stone face, still wondering about it, and down a small embankment to the running stream below. He kneeled, dipping his hand into the cold water, raising it out and quickly sucking the water before it could escape back to its whole. The pain throbbed again in sharp succession with the beat of his heart as he bent over the rushing water. He splashed the icy water on his face, checked his surroundings, and threw the frozen mud onto his shoulder, attempting to numb it.

His belly grumbled, and hunger overtook his senses. His hand plunged into the water, pulling up plants and algae. He stuck them in his mouth, chewing, and plunged his hand into the icy water again. A sweet smell entered his nose, a twig snapped in the distance, and mumbling voices reached his extended ears. His head snapped towards the growing sound, and his body turned as he cautiously made his way up the embankment.

Two men followed a path, holding fishing poles, tackle boxes, and a stringer full of fish. The wind blew against his back and then shifted direction, becoming calm as they approached. They stopped in front of him and looked at each other, breathing deeply and changing the weight of their load between their hands. One of the man's nostrils flared as Roa-Ma squinted his eyes, wanting to move. The man looked at his friend and punched him in the arm. "Good God, Steve, if you're gonna do that, give me some notice."

"I didn't do nothin'."

"Well, it sure wasn't me," the man said with a smile. He slapped his friend on the shoulder, and they proceeded on their way.

What was that all about? Roa-Ma wondered as he paralleled them from behind the rock. He watched them disappear as their voices faded into silence. He crept around the rock, running near the stream's banks and avoiding the trail where he had seen the creatures he wanted nothing to do with.

He continued running along the side of the water. He entered a field, and a lake gleamed in front of him. Fear overtook him, and he ran to a clump of bushes, sitting inside them and trying to clear his head. He spread the bushes, hoping he hadn't been seen, and scanned the banks. Trees partially covered them, starting two or three of his body lengths from the water, and people calmly stood around, holding poles and intently staring at the waves in front of them.

He looked at the mountain range and then at the forest before it. His eyes grew heavy, and his senses faded as he dug into his satchel, pulling out more of the pain-killing leaves and placing them in his mouth.

A human on the other side of the lake screamed as she pulled a fish to the shore. He jumped, thinking he had been detected, and settled down, seeing why the commotion was happening. His mouth watered as she lifted the large trout in the air for all to see. He fought his urge to run after it and closed his bag, chewing on the leaves instead. He stood, grabbed his arm, and dashed further into the trees, putting as much distance between him and the man-made structure as possible.

He slowed his pace, watching the small rock dam fade from view, and looked at what seemed like familiar surroundings. Maybe he had found his way home. Tears came to his eyes as he broke into a full gallop in time to the throb, dodging trees as they steadily passed by.

He spied a small clearing in the distance and circled around. He stopped, leaned against his knees, and hyperventilated as the pain in his shoulder pounded. He breathed in, gazing at the blurry mountains surrounding him, and wished he were home.

He looked in the clearing, double-taking a small group of vines protruding from the ground, and stared at the edge of the trees, timidly entering. He sat, holding his breath from the pain, and exhaled his gratitude as he stripped one of the vines of its red, life-giving berries, shoving them in his mouth.

He snapped the vine at the root, laid it on the ground, and crossed the ends, forming a circle. He grabbed the loose ends, looping them over each other to create a knot, and tightened it. He pulled the circle taut, making sure it would hold, and slipped it over his head.

He placed it around his neck, grabbed his numbing arm, and threaded it through the vine. He relaxed, resting the weight of his arm on the vine. Satisfied it would hold, he pulled out more roots, munched the berries from them, and gave thanks. He made more circles of vines and strategically positioned them around his neck and under his arm.

His arm hung motionless in the homemade sling as he stared into the forest, seeing nothing. He popped another handful of berries into his mouth and slowly moved his hand towards his shoulder, flinching as he touched it. He stood and sucked the clean air through his nose, searching for scents of danger. He slowly turned in a circle, watching the clouds skim across the bright blue sky, and stopped, looking at the trees lining the furthest edge of the clearing from the trail.

He walked to them, knelt down, and dug a shallow grave. He lay in it, confirming it would suit his purposes, and crawled out, raking dirt, branches, and dead leaves around the edges with his feet. He walked through the trees, gathering foliage, and walked to his trench, adding more dirt to the uphill side. He lay on his belly next to the hole and covered his legs and body with the sticks and leaves he gathered.

A fiery pain shot through his body as he extended his left elbow in front of him, laying it flush to the ground. He moaned and sucked air into his lungs, holding it. He quickly moved his body, twisting his shoulders away from his arm and shifting his weight. He whined as he wrapped his fingers around the bone buried deep in his flesh and yanked while pushing the exposed bone inside the skin, bringing them together.

He exhaled an animal-like scream that echoed throughout the mountains as he released his fingers and rolled into the grave. He raised his finger and ran it across the bone. *Perfect set,* he thought, looking at his blurry surroundings. He clawed the camouflage he had prepared earlier on top of him, and the faint odor of a skunk entered his snout as the world blurred, dizzily tuning out.

I-V

John looked at the ham and cheese sandwich Sheila had made the night before and took a bite. Phil busily cut an angle on the last cedar strip, walked towards the house, and put it in place. He pounded in a few nails, stepped back, and looked it over for mistakes. Satisfied, he dropped his hammer through the loop on his tool belt, like a gunslinger would a gun in a holster, and looked at John.

"Not too bad if I do say so myself," he humbly stated, walking towards his boss. He unhooked his belt, tossed it to the dirt, grabbed a sandwich from his bag, and plopped to the ground. We'll get it done today," he smiled, taking a bite from his sandwich and leaning his head back, looking at the sky.

They had been working silently all day, and he knew if he didn't break it soon, it would drive him crazy. He picked up his head, swallowed his food, and looked at John. "Look, man, I'm sorry about this morning."

"Don't worry about it; it's been a little tense for all of us lately."

"No, really, John, I didn't mean nothin' by it. It just sorta slipped out." He took another bite from his sandwich and stared at the ground.

"So, is the siding up?" John asked.

"Yeah, you get the paper down, and the shingles started?”

“Yeah, both sides. Let's finish eating and kick this out today."Okay?" John confirmed as he ate the last of his sandwich and stood, walking towards the box of roofing nails on the ground ahead.

He knelt, grabbed a handful, and put them in the pouch on his belt. He stood, stretching out his body, and looked over the canyon they were sitting above, taking it all in. "So, tell me about last night."

"It was nothin', man. I was sittin' there, havin a couple of drinks and minding my own business when Sandy starts comin' on to me. When I got up to leave, Billy cold-cocked me as I was walking out the door."

John looked at him disbelievingly. "Don't you give me that crap, man? I've known you long enough to know that if there's a woman within ten feet of you, you've got your arms wrapped around her."

Phil looked him in the eye and smiled. "Okay then, would you believe that I accidentally bumped into her, and she asked me to go outside to see her new car?"

"No." They laughed, and John walked towards the ladder leaning against the house.

"Well, there's a lot to do, and we sure as hell ain't gettin' it done sitting here." John looked back over the scenery and then at the distant, ever-present, looming peak.

He thought of an old fishing hole, not far away, that he and a couple of his buddies stumbled onto when they were kids. The fish were biting so hard they couldn't throw their lines out without hooking a sixteen-incher. It seemed like one of the best days of his life.

Phil threw the last bit of chips in his mouth and disappeared into the trees as John stretched one last time before heading up the ladder. He wondered what Sheila was doing and if she had drunk herself into oblivion yet. He stepped onto the roof and focused on his finances and what he needed to do to hustle up the money to pay some of the people he owed.

He thought about going to his father and borrowing from him as he ripped open a bundle of shingles and measured them for his cuts. *No way*, he thought, pulling out his razor blade and slicing the shingles in half and then into quarters. It had been years since he talked to him, and the thought of just walking into his house made his stomach turn.

Phil walked from behind the garage and sat next to the house. John looked down from the roof's edge and placed his knife back in his belt.

"Where in the hell have you been, and what the hell are you doing now?" John asked as Phil reappeared.

"I had to take a leak, and I thought I would sit here for just a minute before coming up. Is that all right?"

"Where'd you take a leak at, the state line?" He impatiently replied as he snapped the rubber straps around the back of his legs, adjusting his knee pads. "I'm almost done on this side, and if you hurry and get up here, I can start cutting the cap. If we hustle, we just might be able to get out of here sometime tonight." He stood and crossed his arms as Phil sighed and stood.

He threw a handful of nails into his pouch and walked towards the ladder. "Okay, okay, no need to panic," he muttered, "I'm getting there."

Phil grabbed the ladder, stepped his foot on the first rung, and John placed his hammer back in his belt as he walked to his pile of shingles. He grabbed a stack, throwing them where he had stopped, and grabbed a full bundle, placing them on Phil's side where he had been working earlier.

He walked to where they lay, put one in place, grabbed a handful of nails, and pulled his hammer from the loop of his belt.

46

He took a drag off his freshly lit cigarette, and Sheila and the kids came to his mind. His thoughts drifted to all the other women in the world and what life could have been as his hammer came down in rhythm, pounding the nails into the plywood below.

He stood, taking the weight off his knees, and stretched his back, popping the vertebrae inside. He climbed down the ladder and walked to the edge of the house, relieving himself of the liquids he had consumed earlier. He refilled his pouch with nails, glanced at the looming peak, and stepped on the ladder. An ear-piercing scream echoed from the mountains, breaking the silence and startling him.

"What the hell was that?" Phil screamed as he ran to the roof's edge, looking at John.

"I don't know," John replied, stepping from the ladder and then back on, expecting it to happen again. His heart pounded wildly in his chest, and the hair stood on the back of his neck. He looked up, squinting his eyes from the glare, making out Phil's torso. "But it didn't sound good."

"Probably just an animal of some kind," Phil responded. "For a minute there, I thought you fell."

"I don't think so," John yelled as Phil disappeared from his view. "I've never heard anything in these mountains that sounded like that before. It sounded like it was in some serious pain, didn't it?" He reached the top of the ladder and stepped onto the steep pitch. He turned his head, still clutching the metal sides, and looked at the mountains, getting no reply.

"Hey, that reminds me," Phil's voice came from the other side of the roof. "Hunting season's coming up in a couple of weeks. Have you made any plans as to where you're going?" He appeared at the apex of the pitch.

"Actually, black powder starts tomorrow. "And yeah," John nodded, "I ran into a couple of guys in town the other day, and they said they knew where a huge herd was hanging out. They guaranteed me that if I went with them, I'd bring back a trophy fit to hang on my wall." He walked to the peak of the roof and sat down, looking at Phil, who had a sad, surprised look on his face.

Phil didn't know the first thing about hunting, and John believed he went for an excuse to drink. Anywhere you would find a party, you would find Phil. John gave him a serious look and began to laugh. "Actually, I figured I would just let you and that nice car of yours drive me back off to the divide where I know we won't kill anything except a couple bottles of whiskey."

"Now, that's the way I like to hear you talk," Phil laughed, "You know, I've been thinking about us never seeing anything, and I wish I could figure out where they all go." He suddenly became serious. "I see 'em all the time when I'm coming back from my sister's, and if you ask me, I think there's something there that warns 'em when we're coming."

"You're probably right," John smiled. Phil pulled his hammer from his belt and disappeared from view. "And someday that something is going to step out from behind a tree and take you home for supper."John laughed, laying the last shingle his side would take and tacking it into place.

He opened another bundle of the roofing material and looked at Phil, who was busily swinging his hammer and tacking the molded tar and rock as fast as he could. He grabbed a stack of shingles and set them next to Phil. He looked at the setting sun, sighing. They would have to finish in the dark, but at least it would get done.

Darkness engulfed Phil's blue car, like a body bag around a dead soldier, as it silently rolled down the street. They had finished another job as hunting season crept closer and had two more to go. They decided to take Phil's car to the Drunken Steer for a celebration drink. One turned to two and two to three. Now, it was almost two thirty in the morning, and they still had another twenty miles to go before they reached John's tiny home.

When they entered the bar, the snow was lightly falling, and now it turned the rays of the headlights into a sparkling white as it dumped in front of and around them.

"So how does it feel to know that another job is complete, on time, and with the absolute finest of craftsmanship?" Phil asked as John stared silently out the window.

"Oh, all right, I guess. I just..."

A figure darted across the road in front of them, and Phil instinctively slammed on the brakes, sliding the car sideways and completing a circle on the ice. He rotated the wheel, trying to correct the slide, and the car headed around again. John jerked hard as his seat belt snapped into place, holding him snugly in place.

The car gripped the soft dirt shoulder and slammed into the guardrail with a loud screech. Phil yelled obscenities, and the car slowed. He slammed the transmission into the lowest gear, pulled the car off the guardrail, and regained control. He found a place to pull over and slowly brought the car to a halt, resting it on the side of the road.

"What the hell was that?" John yelled after sitting in silence for a few moments.

"I don't know," Phil exhaled, unbuckling his seat belt, turning on the emergency flashers, and jumping out of the car to inspect the damage.

John remained in the car, his heart still pounding and his fingers trembling. He unbuckled his seatbelt and crawled into the driver's seat, making his way out the door. He walked around to the passenger side of the car, examining the gash the guardrail had left, which ran the length of the car. "What do you think it was?"

"Who the hell cares what it was? Look at my car!" Phil ran his trembling hand along the scrape, holding down the lump in his throat. "My parents are going to kill me." He kicked the tire and walked back around the car, waiting as John climbed in.

John entered the passenger seat, sighing heavily and positioning himself in the seat. *Probably just a bear*, he thought. *Just a bear*.

Phil slammed his emergency flashers off and rammed the car into gear. He turned it sideways, pulled it from the shoulder, and regained control as the tires grabbed the asphalt and straightened the car. John pulled a cigarette from his top pocket, turned the radio up, and dug a lighter from his pants. He lit his smoke and inhaled deeply as they continued home, shaken and silent.

John crept up the shaky old stairs, hearing the television through the walls. He walked into the living room, stared at Sheila sleeping on the couch, and turned down the television. He listened to her breathing while walking to the chair and exhaled, sitting down, and kicking off his shoes. He lay his feet on the coffee table, got comfortable, and stared at the pictures on the television.

He thought about the creature that had crossed their path. It all happened so fast; there was no way of telling what it was. He knew one thing for sure. Whatever it was, it was walking on two legs. And man was the only animal he could think of that walked on two legs.

A panic struck him. *What if it was a man and they had hit him?* He could still be lying there, hurt or bleeding. Sheila rolled over on the couch and moaned. Her mouth moved as if she were chewing on something, and she became motionless again. He looked at her and paused. She always looked so beautiful when she slept.

I don't know why I'm not a better husband, he thought as the alcohol made him dizzy, and he forgot about whatever it was that could be dead on the road. "I really do have it all: a beautiful wife, two great kids, and a job where I don't have to answer to anybody." He leaned his head back in his chair and smiled. For some reason, and he didn't know why, it was the first time in years that it really felt good to be home.

I-VI

An adolescent deer hopped down a rocky incline. A sharp pain jetted down its shoulder as a blast echoed through the trees. It fell from the impact, tumbled down the hill, stood back up, and started running again. A dried arroyo, densely overgrown with dead shrubs, appeared in the distance. It froze for a moment as a bullet winged by its head and another blast reached its ears.

It sprinted towards the heavy growth, trying to hide from the attack, and stumbled as it entered the rough, dead bushes, slamming to the ground. It thrashed, trying desperately to stand as a sharp pain ran up its leg, and something held its ankle, preventing it from going any further.

The skin ripped as it forced its way up and froze from the pain, breathing forcefully. A voice reached its ears and slowly faded into the distance. It struggled again, trying to free itself, and fell back to the ground. The life faded from its body as it gave up, succumbing to its final breath. Hunting season had begun, the first shot had been fired, and the first casualty had occurred.

He jumped over a large stump like a child leaping over a sprinkler on a hot summer day. The light of the nearly full moon shone brightly through the thick forest, lighting his path. He'd been running since he woke, and the moon's brightness was a welcome sight. He didn't know how long he had been knocked out, but from the looks of the moon, it hadn't been long. He had time to make up.

It felt like weeks. The accident cost him valuable time, and he was sure the season would start soon. He just hoped it wasn't today.

He reached the top of a knoll and headed down the back of the mountain. An itch tingled from his neck and ran down his arm with each step he took. As much as he didn't want to, setting it was the right thing to do. With the bones being back together, it felt like the healing had begun.

He stopped to catch his breath and looked at the moon, which was beginning to cloud over. He bent over, picked up a long, bowed stick beneath him, and looked into the sky. He looked back at the stick and then at the moon. He laughed, remembering his childhood, and pulled an imaginary arrow from his back.

He held the stick parallel to his body, pointed it towards the moon, and placed the arrow into the imaginary string, quickly pulling it back and letting go. He fell to one knee, grabbing his shoulder, and held his breath, waiting for the pain to recede. *I've got to remember that*, he thought as he stood, resuming his journey home.

A small herd of antelope darted in front of him. He hesitated, surprised by the movement, and kneeled down, watching as they quickly disappeared into the night. He looked back at the sky, focusing on the moon. It shone brightly, with two large rings of clouds circling it.

He smiled, staring in disbelief, as the icy wind blew on his face and into his eyes. After all these years of trying, it seemed that it had finally worked. His arrow pierced the clouds and reached its target just when he needed it the most. *Maybe Dad was right after all*, he thought as a smile came to his face and laughter worked its way from his belly.

A large mountain lion grunted as it walked along the same path as the antelope. Its breath turned the cold air to a fine mist, rising above its head and through the moon's rays. It stopped hearing the sounds of amusement and turned its head towards a giant hairy silhouette. The laughter suddenly stopped, and the origin of its beginning disappeared. The lion sniffed the air, turning his head towards the antelope's path, sniffed the air again, and continued after his next meal.

A sigh of relief exited through Roa-Ma's lips as the lion disappeared into the darkness. With his injuries, a fight with the lion could be fatal. The icy air blew hard on his face, and he cautiously stood, shaking the snow from his coat. He glanced around and bolted back on his trail, heading for his home and temporary safety.

The sun rose above the mountains, and the vast line of peaks glittered in the distance. He was almost there. He looked at a tremendous barren meadow that sparkled white and gold as far as his eyes could see. This was the part of his journey he hated the most. And no matter how he planned it, he always ended up here early in the morning. Now, he would have to find other things to occupy his time until the darkness returned, and he could cross unseen.

He looked at the sky and the clouds moving in. It looked like it would be snowing again, *and soon*, he thought as he looked back over the barren area standing between him and his children. There was no way to move now. He knew it would be too risky with the darkening skies and the falling snow. He focused his gaze on the road running lengthwise through the desert.

A flash of light twinkled on the horizon. They were on the move again. They were always on the move. Whether it was the dark of night when the moon shone full or in the middle of the day when the sun burned bright, they were still on the move. That was one thing he would never understand as long as he lived. *Why didn't they sleep?*

He moved deeper into the trees and further from the road, wondering what kind of creature never rested.

The glittering lights drifted behind him as he pondered how he had gotten so far off course and misjudged that jump. Light twinkled in the distance, and a small town came into view as he approached the mountaintop. There was just no way of getting around them anymore. Their race had grown so big while his had slowly become less and less. His father told him of a time when they lived together in peace. A time he couldn't imagine.

This trip home had nearly been fatal. He broke his collarbone and was almost struck by a car as he attempted to cross the stream of stone. He knew that if his carelessness led to something happening to him or if he were seen or captured, their existence would soon be over, and the hunt for them would surely begin.

He could have cost them everything they had worked for through the centuries. He also knew that man, who had been in the process of destroying his world since they had appeared sometime during the beginning, didn't need his help.

He thought of the first attack and of the stories his father told him —the same stories he now told his children. He wondered if the story about his kind being slaughtered and the leaving of the two," who gave rebirth to their kind, was true.

Even though he had seen the destruction, he never believed the story of the first attack or of them living in peace and harmony. He just couldn't imagine a creature capable of doing such things as destroying an entire species. If the "two" had existed, it would have been better if it had ended there, and the instinct of staying hidden had never developed.

Their lands became thinner as man's grew, and now, it was only a matter of time before they destroyed everything and exposed his race. He shook his coat, turned from the town, and walked further into the forest, his only illusion of safety.

The snow fell throughout the day and stopped just as quickly as it had begun. He kept busy planting and started running as soon as the sun set. Now, the moon had almost reached the east end of the sky, and the trees loomed in the distance. A feeling of anticipation overtook him as he realized he would make it before light. His home was a short distance away, and he could almost smell the scent of his son and daughter.

He entered the trees, stopping to catch his breath, and bent over, placing his hand on his knee, trying to slow his breath. *I'm getting too old to run all night like this*, he thought, still panting. He stood, reaching into his primitive pouch, and pulled out a handful of seeds. He kneeled down, planting them at the forest's edge, showing his gratitude for safely getting him across the sandy field and home.

A loud crack echoed from behind him and carried through the mountains. He slipped into the trees, stopped, and lifted his nose in the air. The smell of blood simmered through his snout and into his lungs as the pain of hunger ripped through his stomach. He smelled the air again, zeroing in on its direction, and began running towards it. He kept the scent circulating through his respiratory system as he weaved through the forest, suddenly stopping.

He kneeled and touched his finger to the ground, lifting it and eyeing a gooey substance in the brightening sky. He moved it under his nose and touched it to his tongue. He looked at the blood trickles following the small deer's tracks on the wet ground before him. It sure feels good to be home, he thought as he tracked the path the animal had left.

He looked at a grove of small aspen trees and bare bushes forming a quaky area. He raised his nose, breathing in the smell of gunpowder and man. Whatever was hurt was in the dead bushes. Unfortunately, the man was close, too. He silently walked down the slight embankment in front of him, peering through the bushes, trying to see what it was while keeping an eye on the distance for any movement.

He thought about his shoulder. With all the excitement, he had forgotten about the pain. He scanned the dead branches, focusing on a large white fur ball. His hairy arm reached up as he stepped forward, pulling the bushes and small trees to one side.

A small deer with brownish hair and a white undercoat stood twenty yards in front of him. He glanced at the small horns protruding from the top of its skull and concentrated on its small, infant-like body lying motionless. Its head jerked to one side, and the life slowly ran from its eyes as it glared through him and its surroundings.

A large gash drained blood above its neck, and a piece of barbed wire stuck out from behind its rear leg, pinning it to the ground. Roa-Ma looked at the blood forming a small puddle and knew what had happened. Hunting season had begun, and his world was about to go insane.

The deer froze and stared at the huge torso that towered above him like the mountains that surrounded them. He panicked, trying to stand, but fell back to the earth, still trying to run. The figure's long, gray, and white tinted mustache and beard hung to its waist, and the dark, leather-like, brown skin covering its nose wrinkled around its sky-blue eyes, disappearing into the thick fur that led around its small ears and head. Its body was covered with patches of light brown, dark brown, and grayish hair with tints of yellow and green that thinned as it reached its chest, leaving the same leather-like skin that covered its face and hands.

Its enormous feet sank in the quagmire where they stood, and its right arm hung just below its knees. The other hung in a homemade sling, protecting a leather pouch. Its large chest and shoulders spread the small trees and bushes apart in an intimidating manner, and he could feel it staring at him.

He twisted his head and looked up, feeling like he was in a dream. Its oversized lower jaw and large head looked at him and cocked its head in imitation. With the hair covering its body and hanging over its face, oversized jaw, and brown dog-like pointed ears, it looked like a man, locked away somewhere in the pasture of his mind.

His surroundings faded as it opened its mouth, showing its large white teeth, and slowly approached him. He lay silent and still, succumbing to what he thought would be his final demise.

II
Home

II-I

Trees flew by like mile markers on the highway as the sun disappeared behind the unfamiliar snowcapped mountains ahead. John heaved in and out, feeling like he had been running forever. His eyes scanned the wooded path, and he wondered if his lungs could withstand the strain.

The ground trembled as a booming, hollow explosion echoed around him. He turned, searching for the origin of the sound, and saw a prominent hairy figure with the face of an old man streaking through the forest and heading his way at a fast rate of speed.

A panic pumped his adrenaline as the muscles in the back of his legs tightened. He tried desperately to run faster but fell into a large pile of leaves instead. He flipped back to his feet and stood, questioning the absence of the monstrous being and the sudden stillness surrounding him.

A gust of wind blew through the trees, and the freezing air stung his eyes. He shivered, looking at the sweat and small bumps covering his naked body. It started to snow and instantly turned into a blizzard of epic proportions, whiting out his immediate surroundings. He turned his head, finding the hairy figure almost on top of him, and began running into oblivion, frightened and desperate to get away.

A large yellowish-brown cat stood in his path, growling and showing its large, freshly blood-stained teeth. It strutted back and forth, protecting the mutilated remains of a young woman's body behind it and intently watching his every movement.

His scream echoed through the forest as the cat sprang from the ground. A large hairy hand reached around his body, grabbing his throat and pulling him from the path of the pouncing cat.

John sat up in his bed, grabbing at the hand around his throat, and whimpering as the pressure disappeared. The fear subsided as the darkness engulfed him, and he realized it was just a dream. Cold sweat ran down his face, and the bumps still protruded from his body. He looked at the darkness, with the vivid images still engrained in his brain, and ran his fingers through his hair, wondering where he was.

Sheila sat with a start and flicked on the light, looking at him half-dazed. "Is everything alright?"

"Yeah," he replied, rubbing his head with the palm of his hands, still seeing the creatures from his dream. "Just a bad dream."

"Another one?"

"Yeah." He stood and walked to the bathroom. He cleaned the sweat from his face, splashed cold water on the back of his neck, and stared at his pale face in the mirror.

"Well, I think you should see a doctor about this!" she yelled as she shifted her pillow under her head, slipping back into her slumber. "Get a warm glass of milk," she mumbled, closing her eyes, "Maybe it'll help you get back to sleep."

"I'm not in the mood for a glass of milk," he quietly responded as he walked out of the bathroom and sat beside her. He smiled a let's get romantic smile and wrapped his body around hers, giving her a deep, sensual kiss and whispering, "I love you," in her ear.

She tried pushing him off, and he kissed her again, more passionately. She shoved him again, moving him off of her and slapping him on the shoulder. "Now stop it, John. I'm trying to get some sleep."

"Oh, come on, honey, I was just trying to show you how much I love you."

"Well, next time, try to pick a more convenient time. You always pick the most inconvenient times." She rolled away from him, pulled the covers over her, and sighed heavily. "Now, good night."

He rolled on his back, staring at the ceiling, and the creature in his dreams reappeared in his mind. It had the face of an old man but looked like an ape. It walked on two legs yet was bigger than the largest bear he had ever seen. Visions of it walking in front of Phil's car and the ensuing crash flashed through his mind and exited as quickly as it had appeared.

What a weird dream, he thought as his pounding heart slowed and he breathed in deep. He rolled over on his pillow, feeling rejected by his wife, and grabbed the blankets, tugging them off her and onto him. She yanked them back onto her, and he sighed, closing his eyes.

He woke, slapping the clock on the nightstand. It was six fifteen. He rolled on his back and sat up, throwing his legs over the bed. He walked to the window, pulled the curtains to one side, and looked out. He squinted as the rising sunlight reflected off the snow, temporarily blinding him.

He slowly regained his sight and looked in disbelief. The snow piled up below and on his window, as large flakes fell from the sky, quickly accumulating on the ground. It was a blizzard, and it looked like he wouldn't be making any money today.

He grabbed a cigarette from the pack on the dresser and flicked his lighter, igniting the end of it. He grabbed an old pair of work pants from a pile of dirty clothes beside the bed and walked into the bathroom. He bent over, pulled up the toilet seat, and breathed a sigh of relief as the liquid drained from his body and the smoke exited his lungs.

Hot cinders smoldered, growing a bright reddish-orange as he opened the doors of his wood-burning stove, and cold air blew in. He crumpled up some newspaper, threw it on the cinders, and watched it burst into flames. He tossed in a couple of logs, closed the doors, and opened the air valves. The flames quickly engulfed the inner walls and licked up the metal pipe, heating the metal box and warming the room.

He grabbed another cigarette from the pack on the ottoman behind him and walked to the window, placing it in his mouth. He lit it, clicked his lighter closed, and pulled back the curtains. He looked again at the white powder covering the ground, wanting it to stop.

He cleared the condensation from the window and squinted his eyes, making out his cars. They were buried up to their hoods and not going anywhere. There wouldn't be any work getting done today or tomorrow, either. Christmas was only a month and a half away, and hunting season would start this weekend.

If the weather didn't clear up, he would have to cut the hunting trip short or altogether. Making money to obtain things for his family and keeping his reputation as a man who could get a job done professionally and on time was much more important to him than getting away for a few days and hunting.

And getting away for a few days was exactly what it was starting to feel like. It was hard to get excited about running around the woods, freezing, and looking for something he was beginning to believe he had no chance of killing anyway. Well, at least as long as he went with Phil.

Phil was a big partier who was loud and obnoxious. Anything within a mile of where they camped had to be able to hear him. He sighed for a moment in thought. Even before he hooked up with Phil, he had never seen his prey. Friends he hunted with killed some nice trophies, but he had never seen anything.

He thought about Kirsten and Zach and all the meat one of the small animals would furnish. If he got one, he could feed his family for a year. He thought about putting a deer in his sights and squeezing the trigger.

The imagined deer before him twisted its head, looked at him, and froze. John hesitated. He breathed deep, holding his breath, and the shot blasted in his mind. The deer dropped before him, and he smiled. *No problem*, he thought.

Suddenly, the hunting trip became important again, and he decided to go no matter what. Odds had to be with him this time. And even a tiny deer would make the trip worthwhile and Christmas much more manageable.

The wood in the fireplace popped behind him. He opened it, throwing in a couple more pieces of wood, swung the doors shut, and twisted the handles back in place. He closed the air vent, took another drag from his cigarette, and walked into the kitchen, exhaling the smoke around him.

He pulled the coffee and filters from the cabinet, loaded them into the automatic coffee maker, and filled it with water. He glanced at the clock on the stove. Almost seven. He would call Phil's mother around seven thirty and tell her not to bother waking Phil. He would call back later if the weather broke, but he doubted it would.

He sucked on his cigarette and walked towards the table as Kirsten appeared in front of him. He picked her up, gently removing her rubbing hands from her eyes. "What's the matter, honey? Are you hungry?"

She looked at him, not knowing whether to cry or be stubborn, and shook her head up and down.

"Do you want some cereal?"

She smiled, shaking her head up and down faster, still trying to rub her eyes.

"Okay, I'll tell you what. You go potty, and I'll make us something delicious to eat, alright?"

She smiled and ran down the hall as he prepared her breakfast.

The coffee maker hissed in the background, and the coffee dripped into the waiting pot below. He pushed a bowl of cereal in front of Kirsten and took one last drag from his cigarette. He crushed the butt into the ashtray and looked up as Sheila, looking half dead, appeared from the dark hall.

She sat at the table, running her fingers through her hair, removing it from her face. She raised her hands in the air, yawning as she reached towards the sky, stretching. "Is there any coffee ready?" she wheezed, reaching for the cigarettes on the table.

"Yeah," he responded, pointing towards the coffee pot and looking at Kirsten, who was happily eating.

"Is it snowing outside?" she asked after a lengthy silence.

"Yeah, and it doesn't look like we'll be getting any work done today."

Kirsten grabbed and tipped her bowl, spilling milk all over her and the floor. "Damn it, Kirsten, can't you watch what you're doing?" Sheila yelled as she stood and walked to the sink. "Now you be more careful next time," she demanded as she angrily ran a cloth under the running water, wrung it dry, and tossed it to John. "Is it bad?"

"Pretty bad," John said as she wiped up the mess on the floor, tossed the rag into the sink, and walked into the living room. "Go take a look for yourself."

"Oh my God," she screamed as large flakes of snow blew in as she opened the door. A small snow drift formed at the bottom of the door and fell at her feet. She kicked the snow away, slammed the door, and walked to the table. "Any idea how long it's going to last?"

"I don't know. I haven't turned on the TV yet. Till later today, I guess, but who knows?"

She stared into his eyes. "Do you know that Christmas is only a couple of months away?"

"I know when Christmas is, Sheila."

"So, what are you going to do about your hunting trip?"

"I don't know, Sheila. I really haven't given it much thought and am too tired to do it now. I'm going back to bed, and we can talk about this again when I get up. Okay?' He stood and walked towards the bedroom as she sat, mumbling under her breath and raising her voice as he got further away.

Zach and Kirsten played loudly in the next room as he slowly opened his eyes and focused on the clock. Eleven. He had slept longer than he wanted. He sat up, feeling groggy, and laid his pounding head into his hands.

He slowly stood, walked to the window, and pulled back the curtains. *Well, this is good*, he thought as the snow continued to fall. *This is real good.* He bent down, angrily putting on his pants, and sat in contemplation for a moment before hesitatingly walking to the living room.

II-II

Roa-Ma woke to a black abyss and sat, trying to focus his eyes. He placed his hand in front of his face, seeing only black. He moved it under his chin and put his head on it, exhaling a tired yawn. His head pounded, and a muffled gunshot vibrated through the rock wall.

His head spun as he stood, stammering for a moment before regaining his balance. He walked with his hands held in front of him, waiting for the wall. He touched the cold surface and sidestepped as he followed it.

He stopped, still trying to focus his eyes, listening to the silence. His fingers searched the rough, rigid edge of the rock, and he followed the cave wall. Pain shot through his shoulder as he pulled back some leaves and twigs covering a small hole, emitting a dull light. He dropped to his knees and pushed the covering to the side, exposing a tunnel.

The room barely brightened as a light twinkled through the opening on the other side. A cold wind swirled on Roa-Ma's face, and he stuck his head into the small tunnel, looking up. He arched his back, stretched his muscles, and squared his body to the hole, crawling into the cave.

The darkness slowly brightened as he worked his way through the rock hall on his hands and knees. A light peered through trees and leaves, covering an exit. He quickened his pace, pushed the shrubbery out of his way, and poked out his head, looking for activity. He turned his head, hearing and seeing nothing, and stepped into the large cave, stretching as he stood.

He turned and walked past the maze of tunnels the room contained to the main entrance of his home. He stood at the entrance, moving the growth to one side, and became blinded by the harsh glare of the sun's reflection off the snow.

His eyes adjusted, and his heart pounded in anticipation as he checked his surroundings. He jumped from the cave, landing knee-deep in snow, and dropped to his back, gazing into the sky, remembering doing the same thing as a child. It had been snowing when he'd arrived, and it looked like it continued after he'd gone to bed. His children thought it would be best for him to take a break and rest for a while before returning to work. After this trip, he couldn't disagree.

That was two days ago. Now, his shoulder felt as good as ever. He was rested and felt up to the task at hand. He looked at the sun in the middle of the sky, and another gun blasted in the distance like a muffled cannon. They got closer every year, and he knew that someday, man would discover their home.

According to the sun, it was already after midday. Too late to begin his tracking, so he would have to wait until tomorrow.

He reached for the pouch still hanging around his neck and pulled out the last of the berries enclosed, popping them in his mouth. Considering it was the beginning of the season, it had been relatively quiet. The clouds covered the sun, turning the air bitterly cold. The snow was falling hard and was the one thing that could slow the hunters down.

It evens the odds and gives me more time, he thought as he looked at the pouch and closed it. He looked at the cave, pausing momentarily, and thought of his family, who resided within. He looked at the forest and trotted into the thick trees and brush.

He tilted his head, looking at the falling snow and catching the large flakes on his tongue. The sky turned gray and slowly darkened as the flakes melted in his face and mouth. The storm was getting worse.

All in all, it had been a good day. The storm stopped the infrequent gunfire that had been going on all day, and he found some rich soil that he was sure would allow his seeds to grow. He also stumbled onto a small herd's tracks and knew where they were going. A branch snapped behind him, and visions of him burying his wife flashed through his mind as he jerked around, facing the sound.

His son Sah stood before him, branch in hand, smiling. "You know," he started, taking a bite from the branch, "This wouldn't be half bad if the sap didn't stick to the top of your mouth."

"Don't you ever do that to me again," his father barked as he walked towards him, snatching the branch from his hand and looking at him sternly. "You startled me and almost got yourself killed!"

Sah stood straight, spitting the bark from his mouth. He was a young male ready to enter adulthood. His masterfully built body was almost as wide as Roa-Ma's, and his winter coat showed more luster and shine.

His soft, leather-like skin hadn't taken on the rough, weather-beaten look of his elders, and his eyes gazed a dark, rich brown. His soft skin wrapped around his flared nostrils, bringing out his mother's features, while the rest of him looked like a younger, healthier, taller version of his father.

Their large feet sank into the snow and ice as his father continued his stern gaze. "Where's your sister?" he asked.

"I don't know. She should be home. You didn't look like you'd be going anywhere when we got up this morning, so I started the tracking for you. I've got a good idea where the biggest herds are and where they're headed."

Roa-Ma put his arm around his son's shoulder, pointing him toward the cave, and smiled. "Well, tell me about it on the way home."

Roa-Ma's daughter Shree entered the cave, placing another clump of snow in the basin rock they chipped out long ago, forming a bowl. They surrounded it with leaves, mud, and other various remnants of the forest in a futile attempt at keeping it insulated. They positioned it close to the cave entrance so a ray of sun fell on it, making its contents melt and heat faster. She walked to her rock table, mixing the last berries the patches would yield this year with roots and cactus tops she gathered from the fields earlier, preparing their meal.

Roa-Ma and Sah pulled the twigs and branches from the cave entrance, entering their home. "Son, I don't doubt that the tracks appeared like they were headed towards Echo Canyon," Roa-Ma started as he shook the snow from his coat, "But sometimes the signs aren't always true. I'll go up there tomorrow and take a look, okay?"

Sah opened his mouth to speak, watching his father turn and look at his sister. "Shree!" Roa-Ma excitedly exclaimed, holding out his hands.

"Father." She smiled back, running into his arms. "Are you feeling better?"

"Oh, much, see, this is healed," He stated, attempting to lift his arm above his head. He quickly dropped it, trying to hide the pain, and squeezed her tighter to his chest. "And I'm feeling stronger than ever."

"Good," she purred, stroking his coat with her hand. "I didn't think you would be getting up today, so I went out and collected some food. Are you hungry?"

He nodded yes and followed her to the basin of slush. She picked up a bowl of water she retrieved from the basin before she added the snow and handed it to him. He looked at the extensive salad, consisting of seaweed from the river bottom, roots, berries, and various nuts and seeds. He drank from the bowl, thinking of how good it was to be home. "So, did you enjoy yourself today?" he asked.

"Uh-hum." She nodded as she moved over, dishing him up a plate of food. "I went down to the lake to get these river plants. I know they're your favorite, Daddy, and I saw three does. We ran and played for a while, but a shot scared them away." She handed him his plate and looked at him. "And the beavers are back, working on their dam. I tried to help them as well, but they were frightened too. "I really hate this time of the year, don't you, Daddy?"

"That's right, Dad," His son quickly added, cutting him off before he could speak. "Hunting season started days ago, and you've already lost a lot of time. I think you're going to need some help this year and..."

"I know," Roa-Ma interrupted, still chewing his food. "And you think that you're the one to do it."

"Come on, Dad, my size is as big as yours, and I'm as strong as anyone in the tribe. You'll have to let me grow up sooner or later, and you need the help now.

He looked his son up and down, remembering him as a child. "You can't this year, you're not ready."

"I am too, Dad. I've been watching you for years, and after the condition we found you in when you got back, I'd say you're lucky I've been following you as long as I have."

"You've been following me?" His temper began to rise.

"Somebody had to make sure you were okay."

"My God, Sah, if I ever lost you or your sister, it would kill me." His voice cracked. "I couldn't go through it again.

Sah looked at his father's trembling face and then at his sister, who was quietly watching with a tear rolling down her cheek. He looked back at his father, holding his desire to speak, and looked at the ground instead. He hated his father telling him he couldn't and knew something would have to happen for him to prove he was ready.

He opened his mouth as if to speak and stood, knocking his chair to the ground. He looked at both of them and stormed from the room. Shree and Roa-Ma watched quietly, wishing they could speak, knowing it was best to leave him alone.

Shree cleaned up the kitchen and wished her father a good night as Roa-Ma sat in the light of the full moon, contemplating his life and the ways of old. He told Shree not to leave the cave until the season ended and told Sah he would reflect on his coming to help. He promised himself for a long time that he wouldn't be as selfish as his father was to him. He was trying to put it into practice, but was finding it the hardest thing he had ever done.

He knew the hunters' guns were more humane than the slow, agonizing death of starvation or freezing, but the memories at this time of year were just unbearable. Hunting season always had a way of taking the strong while the weak still suffered. He knew he had failed at keeping them safe and alive in the past and didn't know how much longer his kind could continue. Man would eventually take over the land.

His life had been burdened with the keeping of the forest, especially when the snow would fly. It was their job to keep the animals safe from the hunters who stalked them. It was a futile attempt at keeping the small animals safe, and his days were spent scouring the forest with a watchful eye, alerting them of any danger he would sense. That was until deer and elk season started.

Then his job really became difficult. He would track down select leaders of various herds and ten of the most robust females he could find from each species. The elk were first, followed by the deer. He would watch over them as he directed them to a hidden canyon in the most obscure part of the high country. He would keep them there, monitoring their breeding and watching for the hunters, until the season ended and all the females were with child. It was his race's way of helping the strong and ensuring the reproduction of the race.

Throughout the centuries of their endeavor, most of the animals that made this journey would make their way to his territory, often bringing females with them. It was the ones who knew nothing of his land that he was always the most interested in, and the spike he found on his way home would be one to take for many future seasons. He had learned a valuable lesson about humanity and looked like he would be maturing into a fine, strong male of his species. He had the makings of becoming an exemplary leader with proper guidance.

The trouble was finding him again. He watched him head west after he applied his primitive first aid and freed him from the shackle that would have surely killed him. He hoped he would continue on that path. *If he did, he should be somewhere close to here any time now.*

He thought about Sah. He knew he had learned the ways and that his adulthood rites should have long passed. He thought of when he was younger and tracking with his father. All of the stupid things he had done that occasionally cost them their prey and almost cost them their lives.

They were behind that year for some reason, too. It was their first day out, and they were headed for Echo Canyon at a high rate of speed. He got cocky and cut through a barren field. He dropped as the first shot echoed in the air. His father entered the field, and a second shot rang out, taking three fingers off his hand. Roa-Ma watched the slow-motion occurrence, stunned and in disbelief. His father grabbed him, and they were gone, listening to the yells of the humans behind them.

He leaned his head on the rock behind him, thinking about the day the same carelessness cost him his wife. He knew he would never be able to live if anything happened to his only son. But he had a point. Hunting season started, and it looked like he would need help this year.

His race lost entire species at different times and places. He wanted to ensure he didn't lose that battle again. He hated men for the pain they caused him and for what they were. He dreaded the day the prophecies of old came true and man took over the forests. They would destroy everything that ever was or ever would be, including him and his kind.

He hoped it didn't happen in his lifetime and thought about his son being the one to face the onslaught. He would never succeed, and at the rate they were growing, he knew it was just a matter of time before one of his descendants would face that day. It could very well be Sah.

"We're doomed." He thought as he grabbed a handful of snow and sucked the water from it. An ice-cold chill hit him in the face. He wasn't getting any younger, and this trip home proved that something could happen to him at any time. "*Then what would they do?*"

Tomorrow, he would begin Sah's lessons, and later, he would call for his rites. He threw down the remnants of the snowy ice, deciding he would live with his decision, whether it was right or wrong, and crawled down the tunnel towards the warmth of their sleeping rooms.

He entered the small chamber, trying to see his children on the bedding that lay on the ground below. He reached to the floor, pulled up some dry leaves and grass, and placed them over the opening. He lay down, bracing his back against them, keeping the cold from entering.

With his back taking the cold, the body heat from the three of them always kept them warm, even on the coldest nights. And someday, Sah would have all of this and everything that came with it. He closed his eyes with his troubled mind working overtime, slowly drifting to sleep.

II-III

John's truck groaned as it crept up the side of the steep mountain range, and snow steadily fell, growing heavier as they climbed. Tomorrow was the first day of deer season, and at the speed they were going, it could be hours before they found the old jeep trail leading to the campsite they had used the past few years.

Snow, pushed to the side of the road by snowplows, towered above them, and pieces of abandoned vehicles, stranded in previous storms, stuck out from their covering. *If it gets any worse, we're done*, he thought as the frozen moisture flurried, turning the barely visible road into a blanket of white.

The back tires spun, and the truck slid sideways. *Damn*, he thought, *now we'll get stuck and be shoveling for months*.

He grinded the truck into first gear, skulking up the steep road. His attention drifted from the work he left behind to his wife. He reached for the four-wheel drive gear shift on the floor and pushed in the clutch, yanking it into low. The truck whirred as he worried she would pass out, leaving the kids alone or, worse yet, trying to drive them somewhere. He hated leaving her and wished she didn't have the drinking problem she did.

A horrendous crash involving his Cadillac drifted from his mind, and he thought of her being with another man. The truck bounced, and the four wheels spun, trying to grab the icy road. It whined as John pushed harder on the gas, and it slowed.

More like another man, he thought, thinking of the time in school when he walked in on her kissing Tom Gable. He was going to kill him, but she stopped it from happening.

No way, he thought as they jerked up the road. That was a long time ago. Even if she got so drunk she didn't know what she was doing, she knew he would find out. The only place to go in town was the Drunken Steer, and he knew everyone there.

They had been working overtime, finishing the jobs they started, and were both exhausted. Somehow, the snow stopped long enough for the jobs to get finished, and they had two to start when they returned. He thought about looking for work and visualized himself shaking hands and making deal after deal. Money poured from the ceiling, and his thoughts drifted to the big houses, nice cars, and women it would bring.

Phil slumped in the seat, slowly breathing. With his social life being what it was, the extra hour had taken its toll. He'd been catching up on sleep since they'd started this trip earlier this morning. The tension continued to build in John's shoulders, and the snow began to hypnotize him. He wished he had some company to keep his mind occupied and off his stupid delusions and thoughts.

His eyes squinted as the sun glared off the snow, and he found the trail he was looking for. Somebody managed to get a plow through the heavy drift, and different sets of tire tracks followed the road up and out of sight. *Amazing*, he thought, *even with the snow, there's still going to be a lot of people here. Maybe we're not the only idiots in the world after all.* He laughed.

He pushed on the gas, sliding the truck onto the two-track road. The front tires lifted from the ground and came down hard as he hit a large bump, landing in a hole. They bounced, and Phil's head bounced on the dashboard with a bang. John pushed on the clutch, coasting out of the hole, and Phil's dazed eyes opened wide. He turned his head, trying to figure out where he was and what had happened.

"God damn it!" he yelled, rubbing his head and the lump that was forming there. "Can't you warn me before we take a bump like that?"

"Sorry," John replied, his hands still gripping the steering wheel tightly. But that wasn't there last year." He laughed, released the clutch, and continued up the slippery trail.

"That's all right," Phil mumbled, still rubbing the lump on his head. "But it really hurts like hell."

They inched past trucks, campers, and tents scattered along the side of the route and through the heavily wooded mountainside. They continued on the trail, searching for a place to park when John spotted a small, open clearing.

"This should work," he stated, becoming re-excited about the trip. He looked at Phil with a half-smile, ground the truck into reverse, and backed into the small clearing they would soon call home.

They emerged from the truck, stretching from the long trip, and yawned. John pulled the tent from the truck bed and unfolded it, laying it flat on the ground. Phil rubbed their hands together to warm them, and they pounded long metal stakes through the provided loops, penetrating the snow, ice, and frozen ground. "Well, this year we're gonna kill us somethin'," Phil exclaimed, pounding a stake into the ground. "I can just feel it." He smiled.

"I wouldn't get my hopes up," John responded, "We've never seen anything here before, and I doubt if this year's going to be much different." He pounded the last stake into the ground with his hammer and thought of the jobs he left behind and the money he could be making.

"Phil?" he asked, holding the tent poles he gathered from the back of the truck. "Have you ever thought that maybe the reason we've never seen anything here before is because of all the people who come here?"

"Oh, come on, man," Phil said. You've got to think positive about these things, or you'll never take home a prize."

He crawled into the tent, placing the poles and raising the canvas. John quickly pounded stakes through the end ropes, holding the top into place. "And besides that," he muffled out from the newly formed room, "That's the best part about coming here." He walked out and snapped the vinyl with his finger. "So, let's party!" He screamed loud enough for everyone within a mile to hear. He threw his right fist into the air and walked into the dark, cold night.

John looked coldly as Phil lowered his arm. He walked to the ropes attached to the top of the tent, pulled them tight, and pounded the last of his stakes through the loops on the bottom, giving the tent more support and holding it firmly in place.

Phil grabbed their sleeping bags and backpacks from the back of the truck as John stacked the cooler, kerosene heater, and miscellaneous supplies. He placed his old radio on top of his load and stared at it.

Every year, Phil would run from campfire to campfire, getting drunk with any of the hunters who would have him, while John would sit, freezing and getting mad at the radio because he couldn't find a station that would hold its signal.

"It's good for P.R. reasons," Phil would always say. "If they know we're out there, they won't shoot us." Any excuse for a party, and you would find Phil there trying to start it.

They carried in their supplies and organized them in the tent. John removed his gloves, blowing his hot breath through his cold

81

hands. He pumped the lever on a lantern he brought in and squatted, reaching for the lighter in his top pocket.

"Looks like it's going to be a cold one," he mumbled, watching his hot breath mist. "Hey, work on getting a fire started, and I'll dig out the heater and some grub, okay?" The lantern swooshed, turning a bright orange, lighting up the canvas room.

Phil opened the cooler and reached in, pulling out a beer. "You want a brew?" he asked, handing one to John. "After I build the fire, I'm gonna go see who's here. Don't worry about makin' me nothin' to eat. I'll handle it when I get back." He grabbed more of the frosty cans, stuffing them into his coat and jeans pockets, and smiled as John popped open his container, lifting it to his lips.

His hands stung from the wet cold as he set his can atop the cooler. He rubbed them together and adjusted the small pouch in the lantern to a glowing white, placing his hands near the glass. Phil finished stuffing his pockets, grabbed one last beer from the cooler, opened it, and took a drink. "Later," John heard him say as he disappeared out the door. "And don't wait up for me."

The fire licked orange and yellow flames into the black night. The wood popped, releasing the pressure caused by the heat, and a flurry of reddish sparks scattered toward the stars.

John sat at the fire's edge, watching the embers float and disappear into the dark sky while slowly drinking his beer and rationing the wood they brought. The first time they came here, he searched the terrain for wood and almost froze to death before he found enough to keep him warm. Since then, he brought his own and made sure he had plenty.

Phil's familiar "Ya-hoo" echoed from the distance. John's breath misted and rose above him as he turned his head and looked where he thought the sound originated. *What am I doing here again*? he thought, as a shiver raced down his spine and the cold penetrated deeper into his trembling body.

He picked up another log and tossed it on the fire. "If I were a deer, I sure as hell wouldn't be hanging out anywhere close to this place." He leaned closer to the fire, putting his hands above it and welcoming the heat it provided.

Work crossed his mind, and quickly turned into a deer appearing in his sights. His finger slowly squeezed the trigger, and the deer in his thoughts dropped to the ground. He prayed this would be the year he got his chance to take that shot and save his family's Christmas.

He was around nine when his friend Ray received a bow and arrow set for his birthday. John stopped by soon after, looking for something to do on a summer day, and his friend proudly showed off the new present. They discussed it and grabbed the dangerous gift, setting off on a "*big game*" safari.

They hadn't planned on killing anything, but when John saw the rabbit sitting on the edge of the rock, it was a shot he had to try. He never dreamed that in a million years, he would hit it. When it ran off with the arrow sticking out of its side, the day's events quickly unfolded like a nightmare.

His friend knew he was going to get the beating of his life if they didn't find that arrow, and he cried inconsolably as they wandered around the field. John spotted it sticking up from a clump of debris in the distance and slowly approached. He grabbed it and pulled, trying to extract it from between the rocks it was wedged between.

It shook violently with life, pulling back and forth and twisting in his hands. He panicked, yanking harder, and it screamed a piercing scream. The arrow pulled from the rabbit's body as John fell on his back, like a child whose father let go of a towel during a tug of war.

They ran back to his friend's house and sat in silence, staring at the bloody arrow with the death scream echoing in his mind. He had never been so afraid or felt so much guilt before or since.

He vowed never to play with another toy that could bring death or pain to anything again. Even the guns that tempted the other boys eluded him. The memory of the scream became pushed into the darkest recesses of his mind. While in his teens, his father asked him to go hunting. He never spent much time with his father and didn't like the idea of hunting, but this was an offering he would be forced to take.

He breathed out as the fire popped, scattering more sparks in the sky, and another drunken yell echoed through the trees. He walked to the cooler, lit a cigarette, and grabbed another beer. He belched as he sat on his rock, staring into the fire.

They reached the crest of a mountain and entered a large clearing, staring over the edge of a seemingly bottomless cliff. An endless valley stretched before him, and a grand U, where the mountain range in front of them and the one they were standing on seemed to meet, framing a large snowcapped peak.

John looked in dismay at its beauty, oblivious to his father's presence, until his father's large hand grabbed his shoulder and pulled him to the ground. "Look over there," his father whispered excitedly. He pointed his finger down the clearing and towards the trees.

A brownish deer with large branching antlers was lying in the weeds, sunning its coat. John looked at his father, smiled, and looked back at the deer. He twisted his head, still enjoying the panoramic view over the edge, and panicked as he watched his father pull the gun to his shoulder and peered through the scope.

"Come on," his father whispered as he pulled him closer to the ground.

He swallowed, resting beside him with his heart beating wildly in anticipation of the blast. His father pushed the gun in his hands, wrapped his arm around his neck, and pulled the butt of it to his shoulder. "This could be your first kill, boy."

John looked at him, wanting to say no, and found himself unable to speak.

"Go on, boy, nobody's going to find out." He smiled as John slowly gripped the gun, looking through the scope. "Now take your time and slowly squeeze the trigger," Echoed through his subconscious mind and over his pounding chest. "Remember, the best place to hit him is in the heart."

John swallowed, nodding his head, acknowledging what he said, and looked at the animal. He pulled the gun tightly against his shoulder. His arms became limp, and his stomach tightened as a close-up of the deer entered his eye. He watched his father shoot this gun before, and the fear of its kick swelled tears in his eyes. "I can't!" He cried, trying to hold it steady.

"What?" His father growled.

"I can't," he repeated, holding back tears. "The gun, I don't..."

"What's the matter with you? Are you a little girl? That gun's not going to do anything to you. Now pull the God Damn trigger and don't you miss, or else I'll take you home and..."

Hearing the commotion, the deer stood and froze, cocking its head and looking at John. His father noticed the deer rising and jumped from the ground, bringing his foot back. The gun's explosion echoed through the trees as it jerked against his shoulder, nearly breaking it, and the deer fell to the ground.

"Now that's more like it!" His father yelled as he pulled his stocking cap over his ears and ran towards the animal, pulling out his knife.

John cried quietly as his father stopped, and the buck slowly hopped out of sight.

His father looked back at him. "Where the hell did you hit it?"

"In the heart where you told me to." He cried back as the pain in his shoulder throbbed.

They tracked that deer for over eight hours, and when they finally found him, he was still alive, lying on his side, breathing quickly. John watched as the life slowly ran from its flesh. The bullet wound pierced and exited its stomach. The pain must have been excruciating. Its eyes glossed as his father grabbed it by the horns, raising its head and cutting its throat.

Peace reigned during His military years, but they taught him that killing was a necessary part of life and was needed. Doing it quickly and precisely was humane. He knew his father understood this by the proficiency of that kill. The memories of both hunts had all but vanished by the time he graduated from boot camp.

The bruise on his shoulder eventually disappeared, and hunting only crossed his mind again when some of his army buddies invited him on an expedition they were planning. After he denied the invitation, they brought him meat from one of their kills. They said it weighed over a hundred and twenty pounds after being cleaned and butchered. Zach had just been born, so when they offered again, he accepted.

The lure of the meat attracted him, but the money he spent on equipment and guns kept him coming back year after year. What he wanted for Christmas this year was the thing that had eluded him for so long. To get a buck in his sight and watch its lifeless body crash to the ground.

He thought of how ironic his life was and how much he had changed through the years. He held his watch close to the fire. It was ten. Five would be coming early, and if he were to realize his dream, that was when he needed to be up. He stood, scraping his foot along the ground, pushing dirt and snow on the fire. He walked to the tent, looking back at the darkness and smoke the flooded fire produced. He hoped Phil hadn't passed out and frozen to death as he unzipped the door, walked through it, and sealed the opening behind him.

The heater had warmed the tent comfortably, and he wondered why he had been outside freezing. He kneeled next to his sleeping bag, unzipped it, and sat down, removing his shoes. He undressed and slipped into the bag, zipping himself in. He lay there, moving his feet, trying to warm them, and leaned over to interrupt the fuel source for the lantern. He rolled over, enjoying the warmth, and closed his eyes.

He pulled his sleeping bag over his head as he woke with a freezing wind blowing on his face. He realized where he was and sat up, looking at the snow blowing through the flaps. He grabbed a flashlight, pulled his head into his insulated bed, looked at his watch, and poked his head out, shining the light on the frost forming on the walls.

The light brightened Phil's fully clothed body, shivering on his bed. His mind was oblivious to the cold or anything else going on around him. John was amazed that he found his way home.

Stupid idiot, he thought as he stretched to grab his pants. He wiggled them on inside the warmth of his sleeping bag and grabbed his shirt and socks, putting them on in the same fashion. He crawled out of the bag, threw it on top of Phil, and re-zipped the tent's flaps.

He sat on the cooler, shoving on his shoes and heavy coat. He walked to the heater and quickly refueled and re-lit it.

He thought it was a good thing Phil left the door open, feeling the warmth the heater produced. He had a long way to go and wanted to get there before sunrise. He stuffed a box of bullets in his coat pocket, grabbed a couple of packs of cigarettes, and pulled on his orange vest and hat. He pulled a cigarette from his top pocket, picked up his rifle, and unzipped the door. He cleared his throat, slipped the gun over his shoulder, and stepped out, re-zipping the slit in the tent. He sucked on the end of his smoke, threw it on the snow, and began walking through the trees.

A dim light crept over the mountains as John clambered through waist-deep snow up a steep ridge. He had to hurry. The sun was breaking the horizon, and the plan was to be in position before it was fully exposed. He threw another cigarette to the ground, coughed phlegm into his mouth, and spat it into the snow. He picked up his pace and forced his way to his objective, wheezing rapidly and feeling like his lungs would explode.

He found this place a couple of years ago and wanted to try it since. He hoped everyone had the same kind of night as Phil and would still be asleep. His adrenaline raced as the incline became steeper, forcing him to step sideways up the remaining terrain.

He reached the top of a small knoll, looking at the snow-filled mountainside he had passed through. A gun blasted in the distance and subsided. He kicked the snow off a rock and sat behind it, coughing, breathing hard, and hoping he would be the one to take the next shot.

A stream trickled and disappeared under the snow ahead of him. Anything coming for a drink would have to pass directly in his sight. With the absence of trees within twenty-five feet of each side and the rock, he was hiding behind. A clean shot was almost guaranteed. It was perfect.

He breathed deep, caught his breath, and reached for his top pocket. A branch popped, and trees rustled. He squatted, silently setting the barrel of his gun on the rock, and aimed it towards the middle of the clearing, waiting for whatever it was to appear.

A small deer with spikes for horns and weighing less than a hundred pounds popped in front of him, slowing its pace. John's heart pounded as it reached the stream, lowering its head. He fought the urge to start firing and looked through the scope, placing the "X" between its small, immature horns.

He moved it up and down its tiny body, stopping on its shoulder. It wasn't the biggest buck he'd ever seen, but it would have to do. He breathed in and held his breath, thinking of his smiling children as the mighty hunter brought home his kill.

He paused, breathed out, and lowered his gun. He looked above the scope and watched the deer move closer. A squirrel chirped next to him as he heard his father yell. He raised it again, closing one eye and looking back through the scope. He planted the "X" on his shoulder and held his breath again. *Sorry, buddy*, he thought, *but you're the only hope I've got for a Christmas this year.*

He slowly squeezed the trigger and felt the recoil slam against his shoulder. The small deer dropped, and the blast echoed through the valley.

II-IV

A small coyote pounced through an open field and into the trees. The explosion of a gun echoed through the mountains and into the dusk of the nearing day. The coyote lifted his head from the remains of the rabbit he was chasing and timidly gazed through the forest.

Roa-Ma raised his head, smelling for danger. It stopped snowing during the night, and the shooting would become more frequent as the sun worked its way over the mountains. He scanned the trees and looked at the small deer standing before him. His son worked as if the ways of old were natural, and they rounded up the animals near their home in record time. Now, Sah led the small herd to the Crown of the Keepers while he went looking for this one last male.

The animal he saved on his way home never left his mind, and he knew he had to take the time to see if it stayed on the path he had set before it. He hated the idea of tracking this late in the season, but visions of the only other male he had saved early in its life crept into his mind, and he convinced himself he had once again found that magnificent leader.

In another year, this small animal would mature into a beautiful buck and be the one to help his son when he was no longer able. *I should have at least two or three more good seasons*, he thought, painfully moving his left arm. *And that should be enough time to teach Sah and this little one the ways of the keepers.*

He searched his territory for the past three days and had all but lost hope of finding the immature animal when it loped in front of him. He took advantage of the trust he had built when untangling him from his snare and had been leading him towards Sah since. The wounds had scabbed and were healing well, and since it stayed on this path, Roa-Ma knew he had made the right decision.

When they reached Sah, he would put the buck in the cave with the does, stop by his home to check on Shree, and then see how close man was. They had never breached the perimeter of his territory, but he still stayed close to home during this time of year. He hadn't tracked any animal this late into the season since the incident with his father, and the thought of him being in the forest with hunters quickened his pulse.

He stared through the animal kicking in the snow and looked into the sky. The pain in his shoulder worsened as the days wore on, and he had to slow his pace. The number of animals they had was sufficient, and with the addition of this young male, this season would be as successful as it would get. He figured he was about a third of a day's run to the Crown and could then concentrate on his family's safety as well as the safety of the animals in his territory.

He leaned against a tree, watching the little buck chew its harvest, thinking of all the animals he brought on this journey. His thoughts turned to Shree, and he pictured her safely inside their home. He thought of Sah and of his progress during this pursuit. He was doing well. He navigated the forest so quickly his father had trouble knowing where he was, and his acute awareness of the forest showed his cautiousness.

He still has a lot to learn, he thought, wishing he had been able to spend this time with him. He knew his son was better than he was at his age. Unfortunately, he also knew the dangers involved with the two of them tracking this late in the season. He thought of the explosions the hunters produced, and his thoughts drifted to his wife.

The other male he saved lived in his territory, and they ran through the forest on their way to visit him.

It had only been two seasons since he found the animal, and it became the greatest leader either of them had ever seen. It stayed close to their territory and rounded up the animals needed well before the guns began. His life was falling into place. He had his wife, his children, and a leader who would allow him to concentrate on them.

There was an excitement in the air he hadn't been able to feel since. She carelessly sprinted through a clearing. The sound of the blast echoed in his head, and he replayed the bullet piercing her side, spraying blood and breaking bone and cartilage as it plunged deeper, penetrating her heart. She sprinted towards him, stumbling from the impact, and grabbed his neck, trying to stop from hitting the ground.

He wrapped his arms around her, and she opened her bloody mouth, mumbling something about exposing them, and quickly became limp, slipping into shock. He stumbled and grunted the air from his lungs as he fell to his knees from the jolt. He panicked as he heard voices approach from behind and swung her over his shoulder, galloping through the forest.

Voices drifted in and out as two figures ran, and they tried to keep pace. "What the hell was that?" One of the men yelled, hyperventilating.

"I don't know," the other yelled as they slowed their pursuit. "But I know I hit it."

Roa-Ma raced towards his perceived safety, putting as much distance between them and the hunters as possible. The voices turned to a mumble and vanished as the forest thickened. He slowed his pace, dodging the trees. *It's not even the season,* he thought as he reached the top of a high knoll above his home. He felt a hot sensation streaming down the back of his fur and her lifeless body over his shoulder. "Please, dear God, it's not even the season," he sobbed, falling to his knees.

He laid her down, panicking at the blood trickling from her mouth and covering the side of her body. "It's not the season," he howled as she convulsed, spitting blood with a furious cough. She smiled, lifting her hand to touch his face, and suddenly became still, dropping her hand on his leg.

"Hang on," he wailed, leaning down and placing his head above her small breast. "No," he cried as his face contorted, and he pounded on her chest, listening again. "Please, God..." He placed his mouth on hers, blowing into her lungs. He pushed on her chest, blowing in her lungs again. "Please, dear God..." He cried, repeating the procedure again and again. He held his breath through his tears and placed his head back above her breast, still hearing nothing. "It's not even the season!" He screamed, looking into the sky.

Tears rolled down his face, and his bottom lip trembled. "You can't leave me," he mumbled in her ear. "You just can't." He leaned back, detecting his own blood-stained body, and stood, screaming between sobs. He looked at her, jumped to his knees, and again listened to her heart, holding his breath and praying for some kind of sound. He pounded on her chest, feeling the shock of his loss and refusing to give up.

The small buck lifted its head and hopped through the forest. The movement startled Roa-Ma, bringing him to the here and now. He jerked his head, following the animal with his eyes, and sprinted after it, cutting it off as it wandered off course.

Most animals understood what he was doing and felt it an honor. However, the youth in front of him didn't seem to be aware of what was going on and became aggravated when Roa-Ma tried to stop his directional inconsistencies.

He wondered if this was the way it had been when his race first became aware of the reason for their existence and began making more intimate contact with the animals. This instantly evolved into a sometimes futile attempt to protect the helpless and ensure their existence. He thought about the first to know this was their purpose and questioned if they got it right.

He glanced ahead at his familiar surroundings and felt a sense of safety as they entered his territory. It was lucky he found the animal when he did. With its youth and disregard, he thought it likely it hadn't remained on the path he placed him on. He was ready to call off his disappointing search and head home.

Now, it seemed as if fate brought them together again so he could give him the proper guidance. This animal could live up to its potential and become what it was born to be. It felt as if his wife was keeping an eye on him, and now he just had to get the toddler safely to the Crown.

The more the guns fired, the more the animals feared, spreading throughout the lands, making it difficult for the hunters to turn them into prey. *They would adapt until the very end*, he thought, as his shoulder ached and he began feeling fatigued. Home sounded better and better as the moments passed. He looked at the pointed peak leering in the distance and then at the pale sky. *There's no way we'll make it before dark*, he thought, visualizing his son's face after he made his way through the maze of the Crown with the buck safely in tow.

It was a beautiful place, never visited by anyone except his race, animals needing help, and the occasional curious observer. The scent of man had never spoiled it, and the nearest river of stone was at least a full day's run. Its sheer rock cliffs surrounded its basin and towered above the ground, making it look like a dazzling fortress that was impossible to reach from the bottom. No hunter had ever ventured towards it, and he prayed no civilization would ever attempt to conquer it.

A large room lay inside the cliffs, making a small, narrow valley that could only be entered through a maze of caves that labyrinthed through the stones. At the end of the valley, another maze began. When properly navigated, this maze led to a small opening, which led to a large room that stretched as far as his eyes could see in all directions.

The rocks curved at the top and stopped, allowing the sun's rays to shine in and the vegetation to flourish year-round. The walls acted as shields, blocking the cold and wind, and forcing the heated air they produced through the top. The snow never became deep, and although soft blue ice covered the inside walls, the temperature was always warm and comfortable.

A small amount of wildlife would be able to live there forever, never worrying about freezing or starving. If necessary, it could fit an entire herd and sustain them for the duration of their lives. It was the room God had ordained where all species, including his, would make their final stand.

It was a shame the animals suffered because of man, and historically, man was always the most aggressive and cruelest of the animals to inhabit the earth. They created their instruments of transportation and death, systematically destroying each other and their surroundings. Now, the deer, with no defense at all, had to run for its life every year.

It was time to pick up the pace. He lifted his arm, looking ahead in anticipation of his smack on the buck's rear. A panic overtook him as he stopped, looking over the fresh virgin snow. The buck was gone, and there was no sign of his tracks. *Great,* he thought. The sun would be rising above the mountains soon, and a tribulation was playing out in front of him. The only way to end it was by finding this buck and getting it to its destination.

He looked at his tracks in the snow and broke into a jog, following them. He reached where the buck's tracks veered in a different direction, pursuing a random path. Fresh fecal matter with steam rising from the top lay on the ground beside him, and the tracks wandered, entering a clearing. If he were going to survive in this world, he would have to learn that being exposed was no way for a male of his species to behave during this time of the year.

The older bucks learned at a very young age that when the guns began blasting, it was better to stay hidden and to travel with females. Males were the primary target, so the females would enter the clearing first, allowing them to stay near the edge grazing, ready to bolt at the first sign of trouble. It wasn't the most efficient way of doing things, but after watching their parents and friends get shot, it was the only way they knew.

He reached the edge of the clearing and peered through the trees, staring at the spike still kicking the ground in search of food. *What a shame we have to learn how to live and how to die*, he thought, feeling calmness and a sense of success at finding him.

A breeze hit him in the face, his nostrils engorged, and the inside of his stomach twisted. There was a man somewhere close. Too close. He pointed his nose in the air and breathed in, smelling nothing. A false sense of security surrounded him, and his anxiousness to get the buck into the trees overtook him. He stood straight, walking into the clearing.

The wind shifted direction, and the scent of man became unbearable. He dropped to his knees and began imitating a squirrel's chirp, sending a warning to his companion. The buck cocked its head, looking in his direction as the trickling of a small stream faded in from the distance. Its head dropped, and it turned toward the stream, prancing toward it.

II-V

The spike froze, and Roa-Ma fell to the ground. A gun exploded, and the world slowed. Meat and blood splattered as the bullet entered the shoulder of the deer and continued through its body. Its front legs buckled as its lungs filled with blood, and it dropped to its side, cracking ribs and forcing the red fabric of life from its nose and mouth. Its blood drained as it kicked, desperately trying to stand, and fell back to the ground.

Roa-Ma stared in disbelief as visions of his wife's bloodied body flashed through his mind, and he held back his instinct to run to the animal and remove it from the clearing. The deer's head jerked, and its eyes clouded as it entered a dream. The adrenaline stood him up, and his front legs gave way, dropping him back into a pool of his own steaming blood. Everything became blurry, and life rose from his body as an adult-sized figure noisily approached.

John jumped from the ground, throwing his fist in the air, celebrating his victory. His hands shook from the adrenaline pumping through his body, and he raced towards the deer. He slowed his pace as it stood, quickening it again as it slammed back to the ground.

He stood by the infant's side as blood escaped from its nose and mouth and the life drained from its soon-to-be corpse. He propped his rifle against the nearest tree and drew a large knife from the sheath strapped to his belt. The spike pointed his head towards him, giving a final look of despair. *Why are you doing this to me?* He thought he heard it say as it tilted its head and looked at him. Its head dropped to the ground, and it moved no more.

A tear rolled down his cheek as he looked at his knife and then at the lifeless body of the deer. He grabbed the animal's muzzle, pulling it back forcibly, exposing its neck. "Sorry," he mumbled, putting his blade to its throat, "But we really need the meat."

The razor-sharp knife cut through the flesh, leaving a long, gaping slit, and the remaining blood clotted on the ground, turning the remaining white snow a deep red. He dropped the deer's head and stepped back, gasping from the deed. He walked to its hind quarters, held the back legs up, and spread them apart.

A movement flashed from the corner of his eye, and everything became unbelievably real. His heart beat rapidly, and the adrenaline flowed back through his veins. A cold chill ran the length of his spine, and he crouched, reaching for his gun. The branches rustled in front of him, and a low growl ran through the clearing. He stood as motionless as the deer beside him, watching a figure dart through the trees, snapping branches and rustling through the snow. Something stalking the deer, he thought as the growl started through the clearing again.

He lifted his rifle, placed it against his shoulder, and slowly turned in a circle, covering the clearing in anticipation of the impending attack. *If it's the deer it wants, it'll have to take it from me*, he thought. *This one's for my children, and nothing's going to take it away.*

A squirrel chattered in the distance as the growl became louder and suddenly stopped, leaving his environment perfectly still. The figure sprang from the trees, pouncing towards him like a cat after a bird. His eyes grew wide with fear. The figure registered in John's mind, and the gun recoiled against his shoulder. The figure flew backward, landing on its back, and the reverberation echoed through the valley.

The bullet pierced Roa-Ma's shoulder and shattered, spreading through his chest. The force of the bullet pulled him from his feet, jerking him in the air and forcing him backward. His back numbed as part of it was removed by exiting fragments, and blood gushed down his fur. He hit the ground with a thud and rolled to his feet, screaming and grabbing his now-useless arm. He disappeared into the trees as fast as he had appeared.

Hot sweat flowed from John's trembling body, freezing into his clothes and running down the back of his neck as he looked into the trees, waiting for another attack. *"It was the face from my dreams and the scream we heard at work."* He unwillingly realized as he calmed down and cautiously walked to the blood-stained snow where the figure had been thrown.

Large feet imprinted the snow, and blood splattered everywhere he looked. "Well, this sure as hell ain't no dream," he mumbled, still in shock from the incident. He placed his shoe next to the animal's print and compared their size. It was double his length and width and had the same five toes as him. He squatted, touching the inside of the print, and put his finger in the blood. *I've never heard of any Bigfoot around here.* He thought as he pulled his finger from the blood and rolled it between his thumb and forefinger, staring through the forest. He remembered the dead spike behind him and snapped his head around, looking at it.

His feeling of victory returned, and he fantasized about how happy his wife and children would be when he came home and presented his prize. He looked at the blood-stained footprints of his attacker and stood, searching the trees. Whatever it was, it was hurt, and it wouldn't have a chance of making it very far.

He re-scanned the forest, listening for a sign of the animal, and walked to the spike, pushing its lifeless head with his foot. Guilt set in, and he felt compelled to track down the other animal and put it out of its misery. *It's the least I can do*, he thought as his freezing hands trembled and he reached for the carcass.

The tiny legs pointed stiffly into the air as he rolled it on its back and grabbed its testicles. *We'll see what it was soon enough*. He thought as the knife quickly sliced off the small sack, and a hiss of warm air exited.

Thoughts of his father cleaning the buck he killed as a child plagued his mind. The smell of the exiting gas registered in his brain, and he stuck the knife where the testicles had been, ripping a clean incision in its belly and stopping at the ribs. A cloud of steam rose from the large cut, and he grabbed for the hatchet inside his coat. He rubbed the dripping phlegm from his nose and raised the hatchet into the air, bringing it down on the bones and cartilage, breaking them to the neck. He was just a kid then and always looked at the beauty in things. Not killing them.

It's funny how life changes people, he thought as the hatchet fell again, severing the head from the carcass. Intestines, blood, and organs lay on the ground from the slit in its belly as he held up the head, fantasizing about where it would look best in his home.

He gagged as the intestines gave movement one last time, leaving their odor in his nose and forcing him to turn his head. He breathed deeply, held his breath, and stuck his hands inside the deer, pulling the rest of its insides to the ground.

Pain tingled up his arms, and the feeling returned to his frozen hands as he pushed them inside the deer's warm body, holding them there and rubbing them together. He reluctantly removed them from the carcass and stood looking at the pool of blood and organs. He breathed fine clouds of mist into the frigid winter air. *God, this is so disgusting*, he thought.

He grabbed the animal's front legs, pulling it and its head towards the trees. He dropped them in the snow and knelt, moving the frozen water over the eyes and body. The blood washed from his hands, and they became numb again as he stuffed the carcass full of the icy substance. He slipped his hands inside his sleeves and pushed more snow over the body, attempting to bury and camouflage it.

It wouldn't keep the animals away, but it would keep the meat from spoiling. He put his hands between his legs and rubbed them together, trying to warm and dry them. He pushed them down his pants, enjoying the warmth, and walked to the clearing, slipping on his gloves and grabbing his gun.

He found the large footprints leading into the thick trees and sighed, his teeth chattering and his body shivering. He put one foot in front of the other and slowly trudged off, following the creature's tracks. *I've got to pack that spike and get it back to camp before dark*, he thought as he tugged his wool hat back over his ears. "And I'm really not in the mood to go on some wild goose chase halfway to hell and back looking for some giant, unknown animal that's wounded and not in a good mood anyway."

He had finally talked himself into going back and packing out the buck as the tracks wandered into a clearing, branching in three separate sets, going in different directions. His heart raced, and the air felt colder. His eyes followed each set out of the clearing and into the thick growth as far as he could see. He scanned the area, feeling somebody or something watching him, and cautiously approached where the prints split.

He knelt, grasping his rifle, and stood, ready to shoot anything that moved. His eyes squinted, trying to take the glare off the snow, and he jerked to his left, seeing a shadow in the trees. He stood intently staring in that direction and walked backward, expanding his search in all directions.

A stick cracked in the distance, and a bird began to sing. John snapped around with his gun cocked and bumped a tree, startling himself and firing a shot in the air. The recoil forced him to the ground with a thud, and a pain stung his tailbone. He breathed a sigh of relief as the pain subsided, and he relaxed, reaching for his gun and looking at the trunk. He slowly stood as his eyes followed it into the sky.

A figure jumped from what seemed like the top of the world and floated in slow motion, landing on top of him. He lay in a dream-like state as blood trickled down the back of his neck, and everything turned black.

II-VI

Phil stepped from the tent and looked into a clear blue sky through half-closed eyes. The bright sun forced his head to pound harder and his eyes to squint tighter. "God, what a night," he mumbled. He looked at his watch and poked his head back through the flaps. His sleeping bag, gun, orange vest, and hat lay inside.

Doesn't look like I'll be getting any hunting done today, he thought, bending over the cooler, pulling off the lid, and reaching into the icy liquid. "Maybe John'll have some luck and be in a partying mood when he gets back." He pulled out an icy, wet can of his favorite beverage and pulled the tab, allowing the pent-up carbonation to escape. "Hair of the Dog," he laughed as he placed the can to his lips, and another gun blasted in the background. He held his head with his free hand, sat on a rock John positioned near the fire the night before, and took a drink from his beer.

His bloodshot eyes looked at the white, sparkling mountains before him and the thousands of trees lining the higher mountains. He looked at the beer in his hand and guzzled the contents, throwing the empty container into the smoldering ash.

He propped his elbows on his knees and rested his head in his hands as his headache began to subside. He stood and walked to the tent, spreading the flaps and falling on his sleeping bag. A bird chirped, and another answered in the distance. He closed his eyes and faded back into his world of dreams.

He woke to the sounds of a small war in the distance and rolled over, looking at John's empty sleeping bag. When he woke from his nap the day before, the sun was setting, and John still hadn't returned. He wandered through the other camps looking for him and asked everyone to meet with him in the morning so he could form a search party and find out if anyone had seen him. Everybody knew the people around them, so every person within a five-mile radius would be there.

The gun blasts meant the sun was up, and everyone who came to his meeting would have left thinking he wasn't there because his friend had returned. *How could I be so stupid and miss the group like that?* he thought, reaching to John's sleeping bag, patting the nylon and earth beneath it. He wiggled out of bed and quickly slipped on his clothes.

He reached into the cooler and pulled out the milk he had brought to go with the donuts he had started eating the day before. He took a drink, set down the carton with one hand, and grabbed a couple of the small donuts with the other, popping them through his lips. He took another drink from the carton, held the milk in his mouth, and chewed the donuts, swallowing. He slipped on his socks, retrieved more donuts, and stuck them between his teeth. He took another drink and stared at his shoes as he sat, breathing heavily and chewing.

He laced his shoes, pushed the tent's flaps apart, and walked outside. He looked into the valley and breathed in, rubbing the sleep from his eyes. He put his hands in his pockets and walked towards a large rock. *I'll just sit here for a few minutes and catch my breath before I start looking*, he thought, reaching the stone platform. He sat on it and lay on his back, looking at the sky. I should have brought a beer. His mind drifted as he closed his eyes, and the sound of the wind raced through his mind.

"Hey, wake up," a voice rang in his ears. "Hey!"

He opened his eyes, looking at his friend Ted. "Oh wow," he said, sitting up in shock. "What time is it?"

"I don't know, late in the afternoon, why?"

"I don't know," he looked around, "Is everybody gone?"

"Gone? They're all starting to come back. Um, you don't look so good, man. Your skin's starting to turn blue. Don't you think you should go to your tent and warm up or something? How long you been here?"

I don't know. I don't think for very long." A twig snapped in the distance, and voices approached.

"Hey," Phil yelled.

The men nodded and continued walking.

"Listen," he yelled again, standing and trotting to them. "My friend didn't come back from hunting yesterday, and I was wondering if any of you had seen or heard anything odd over the last couple of days."

The men looked at each other and shrugged their shoulders. "No, nothing odd." One of them answered.

"But we'll keep our eyes open." The other replied.

"Thanks," Phil smiled, "He's a little guy with brown hair, and his name is John."

"Well, we'll let you know if we see anything," The first man said, turning to continue on his way.

"Is that your camp over there?" The other man responded as his friend stopped and watched as the other man pointed at Ted's tent while glaring at them.

"No," Phil answered quickly, "I'm up the road a ways and on the right."

"Well, if you know them, you tell them that if their partying keeps us up at night and scares away all the animals, we're gonna come have us a little talk with them." He coldly changed his look from one to the other in silence.

"Well, if you do, give them some for us," Phil piped in, "The bastard's been keeping us up since we got here."

"No doubt we will," he said, throwing his gun over his shoulder. "'No doubt we will.' He turned, following his friend towards their camp. Their voices grumbled, and they walked up the road, looking back at them, disappearing into the trees.

Phil walked towards his tent, with Ted close behind. "Give them some for me," Ted mimicked as Phil laughed and fell in step with him.

Ted looked at his tent and then down the road as the two men stopped and looked at them. "You know, maybe it wouldn't be such a bad idea to find somewhere else to party for a while," he said, smiling at Phil and watching the men disappear.

"Not," they screamed in unison. They laughed and continued on the road to Phil's canvas hut.

Phil shivered as his hands and face thawed. He took a drink from the hot coffee Ted gave him and cupped it in his hand, absorbing its warmth. "I'm really worried about John," he confided, "And I'm gonna have to go into the mountains and see if I can find him."

"I know," Ted returned. "And I looked for him today, too." He walked to him and put his hand on his shoulder. "But I'm sure everything'll be all right." He gently slapped Phil on the back and walked from the tent.

Phil stepped from his tent and looked at the mountain with ravines resembling saddles sitting on the left. John told him the saddle furthest on the right, past the small range in front of him, yielded a river and a clearing big enough to get a clean shot at anything coming for a drink. He had been trying to get there every year, positive he would get a trophy worth mounting, but he never made it.

Phil, unfortunately, had never been anywhere close to it. Too many late nights to make those early morning jogs. He put his hands in his pockets, walked to his tent, and grabbed his orange vest and hat. He picked up his gun, ensured it was loaded, and snatched a beer from the cooler.

He looked at the saddle's distance and popped the top of the can. *Sure looks like a long way*, he thought. He stopped, walked back to the cooler, and grabbed a couple more beers, stuffing them in his vest pocket. Satisfied, he began walking towards the location John had talked so much about.

He breathed heavily, kneeling over a set of footprints, and prayed they were John's. He rolled on his back and grabbed his side, trying to breathe. *God, that last hill was too much for me*, he thought, looking at the tops of the trees. He rolled to his hands and knees, hyperventilating, and leaned back on his legs. "I knew I shouldn't have drunk that last beer."

He grabbed a handful of snow, squeezing the moisture from it into his mouth. He felt lightheaded and nauseous. A hot flash produced beads of sweat on his forehead, and he dropped to his hands as the foam from the beer he had consumed jetted up his throat, projecting onto the ground.

He compacted a handful of snow and threw it in his mouth, sucking its moisture. He rolled on his back, wiped the sweat from his forehead, and breathed deeply, slowly exhaling. His breath returned, and his body temperature dropped. He took another bite from the icy snow, lowered his head to the ground, and lay there watching as the clouds floated through the sky. *The rest has got to be easier than this*, he thought. *Following these prints should take me right to him.*

He continued as the tracks entered a small treeless valley with a stream running through the center. He followed the tree line left and then back to the right, scanning his surroundings and looking for any sign of his friend. Various animals' tracks covered the clearing, running over a blood-red stain in the snow. Oh my God, he thought, running to the bloody mess with visions of John being shot by another hunter screening in his mind.

The blood smeared through the snow and towards the trees. Phil followed the trail, finding a small deer's snow and leaf-covered body. The birds had been picking at the carcass, and only a boot print remained, imprinting the snow between its spiked horns. "*They've got to be John's*," he said to himself as he looked back over the clearing, wondering if more of the prints could be found.

He blocked the sun with his hand and looked at the ground. "*Where the hell did all of these prints come from?*" It looked to him like every animal in the forest had stampeded through this clearing, taking any explanation of the incident with them.

He followed the stampeding prints into the forest, where they broke up, scattering through the trees. He scampered to where he first entered and found the bootprints of the hunter before they became unintelligible, covered by the mad dash of prints. He walked, scanning the edges of the clearing, stopping periodically to walk into the forest.

He spotted two sets of prints exiting the clearing and followed them as they came together, forming a thin line through the trees. He looked back over the clearing and then at the tracks before him. *Then*, he thought, *let's see where they go*, following them through the trees.

The tracks branched into four and scattered in different directions. His eyes followed the smallest set, leading to an orange cap glowing in the white snow. *Oh God*, he thought as he ran towards it, picking it up. It's John's.

He stood, looking back at the three sets of large tracks, and followed each one as far as his eyes could see. A patch of red glimmered in the distance. He trotted towards it, looking at John's blood-stained hat in his hands and the red patch below. He looked at the tracks and followed one about a hundred yards into the forest before it just stopped. He searched at least ten yards in each direction, but they never started again. He repeated the procedure with the other two sets, finding the same results.

This is crazy, he thought. *Nothing could just disappear like that*. He walked back into the clearing, looking for tracks, and exited, finding nothing. He turned, looked at the sun's position in the sky, and followed his footprints back to where he started.

Phil opened his tent and stared at the still-dark mountains. The sun crept over the mountaintops, gradually lighting his surroundings. He looked at the police cars parked along the side of the road and the helicopter in the clearing. It started its engines with a whir, and the blades began slowly spinning, picking up speed. Police officers stood around a large fire, sipping coffee and warming themselves against the flames as the helicopter roared and lifted into the air, flying towards the mountains from which he had just returned a few days ago.

He searched until dark and was lucky he found his way back to camp. As soon as he returned from the confusing scene, he drove to town and called the police. He met them the next morning, making the hike again. That was three days ago, and they were still far from answers. He reached the captain and put his hands towards the heat. "Have you heard anything new?" he asked.

"You know, it's the damndest thing I've ever seen," the officer replied with a sober look. He was an older gentleman, nearing fifty. His hair had started to gray, and his eyes were a deep coal-black. His mustache wrapped around his top lip and ran to his chin, while his potbelly protruded from his uniform. He turned, looking at Phil, and moved closer to the fire. "We know that a deer was shot and gutted by someone, and we would like to assume it was your friend."

"Yeah."

"Well, I was up there myself, and I'll be damned if the snow hadn't melted before we got there." He looked into the flames and stepped back from the heat. We didn't find tracks like you described, Mister Sutherland. All we have is a missing person.

"So, what are you trying to say?"

"I don't know," he said, "you said you were there three days ago, right?"

"And a couple of days ago with your men."

"And the blood sample you gave us seems to be the same type as your friend's, according to his medical records. But we don't have a body." He turned and looked into Phil's eyes. "The only other footprints I can find up there are yours."

"Are you trying to say I had something to do with his disappearance?"

"No," he replied, surprised at Phil's defensive posture, "But let's say for a moment that your friend ran into this clearing, took a bump on the head, and got hurt. When he came to, he couldn't remember who he was and wandered off."

Phil breathed in, attempting to say something.

"Or maybe he decided this would give him a chance to make a new life for himself. Maybe he set the whole thing up, and you're helping him. Or maybe you went up that mountain together, and you know exactly what happened to him. Maybe you just don't want to talk about it yet."

"John wouldn't do that, and I have nothing to hide," Phil stated boldly. "When I first showed your men where I was, the tracks were there. And John's got a wife and kids at home, and he's my boss. He has everything that a man could want. Why would he leave that?"

"I don't know why a man does anything," the captain replied. Maybe it had something to do with that Sasquatch that's been reported around here." He smiled condescendingly, getting closer to Phil's face. But one way or the other, we usually find the truth." He turned his back and started walking towards the fire.

Sasquatch? Phil thought as he headed for his campsite.

The officer stopped, turning and looking at him. "Oh, and Mister Sutherland..."

"Yes," Phil huffed, turning to face the officer.

"Don't be going too far away when you get home. We'll want you to come down to the station, and we'll have some more questions for you. We'll let you know when this gets figured out, and we don't need you anymore. Okay?"

"All right," Phil said, "But do me a favor and let me tell his wife."

"Why would you want to do that?" The captain walked closer to him, developing a new theory in his mind. "You got something for her?"

"Listen, I think it would be better if it came from someone she knows."

"Don't worry about it, son. We'll take care of it."

"No, I insist," His voice cracked as he became emotional, "She'll handle this better from a friend."

The captain stared into the fire, thinking of how classic this was and how truthful his theory was becoming. "All right," he stated, smiling in pleasure and shaking his head. We'll give you until tomorrow night, and then I'll send one of my men over." He turned and headed towards the tent they called headquarters. Phil turned and started back to his camp.

Oh God, he thought, *what will I tell her*? *I don't even know what happened*. He put his loose camping gear in the back of John's truck and began pulling the tent stakes from the ground. He folded the tent, threw it in the truck, and looked back over the wilderness, stopping at the glowing fire in the distance.

He would have a long ride home to think about it. He climbed into the cab, grinded the truck's gears, and started down the road.

II-VII

The snow silently fell as Sah and Shree busily collected roots, leaves, and mud to apply to their father's back. Shree scanned the meadow, spotting the plant she was looking for, and sprinted towards it. She dropped to her knees, dug up its roots, and held them in the air, looking at them through the dim light the sun produced from behind the clouds.

These will be for the man, she thought as she put them in her pouch, which included her collection from the day.

Sah stood behind her and smiled as she looked at him and turned to go. "Why do you think Dad wanted us to bring that thing home?"

"I don't know," she replied, still searching the forest, "But I'm sure it's for a good reason."

"It was trying to kill him. He should have let us kill it then and there and been done with it."

"Don't say things like that, Sah. We're supposed to help things, not kill them. Remember?"

"I know, and we're also supposed to stay away from their kind. Sit back and watch them as they destroy our world. Get real, Shree. Sometimes you have to kill in order to survive, and this is a matter of survival." He stared at her deep, contemplating eyes. "Do you remember when the bear attacked us and tried to take the cave?"

"Yes," she answered, nodding and looking through him with memory-filled eyes.

"We had to kill it, so what's the difference? I say we go in there and kill this right now before it heals and tries to kill us." "No, Sah, I won't let you do that." She looked him in the eye and started running toward their home. "Daddy said to keep it alive, and that's exactly what we're going to do."

She laid her leaves and roots on the solid rock table and grabbed a flat stone, crushing the dried foliage between it and the polished surface.

Sah followed her through the trees and entered the cave. "Why did you run away like that?"

"Father told us to take care of him, Sah, and that's what I'm going to do. You know, if you remember right, the bright idea you and Dad had about killing that bear almost killed both of you. You knew I thought it was wrong to kill him, and I know we could have talked him out of the cave if we had just taken the time. I think studying this man is something that needs to be done, and he could be the one thing that can stop what's written in the scrolls. I think Father agrees."

"That bear could have killed all of us. And if we would've done it your way, it would have!" He answered back. "That...That thing in there will never be able to change anything, and it needs to be killed."

She looked at him and pounded harder on the roots, twisting the flat rock and pulverizing the medicinal properties into a powder.

"Look," Sah started in a soothing voice, trying a different approach. "We've got a real problem here, and I think we need to face it." He looked at her teary eyes, knowing she didn't want to confront this reality. "If Father dies, we'll have to kill the man, and you won't be able to stop me then." He tightened his jaw, trying not to show his anger. "And I vote we do it now!"

"And what if Father heals and asks where the man is? What will you tell him then, Sah?"

"We can tell him he was too sick to save and died."

"Then you should have killed it before you brought it home!" she yelled, tired of the conversation. She discarded the skins and uncrushed pieces from the organic powder, scraping them onto a large rock. Next to it, she laid wet, green leaves and plants from the river bottom, placed a bowl of water on the tray, and walked towards the tunnel leading to the sleeping room.

She stopped, looking at her brother. "I won't let you do it, Sah. If Father dies, you do what you have to do. But if he lives and something happens to the man, so help me, God, I'll tell him you did it and how." She dropped to her knees and crawled into the burrow leading to her father.

"You wouldn't do that," he yelled as she disappeared into the dark hole. "I know you wouldn't." He threw a rock at the wall and looked at nothing. He turned, walking from their home and into the cold night air.

The room's heat increased as Shree worked her way through the orifice. *The fever he has must be terrible to be warming the room like this*, she thought. The heat would help dry the medicines she prepared, hastening the healing of their wounds. Maybe the man would serve a purpose after all.

She entered the room and looked at the man, shaking, shivering, and mumbling unintelligible sounds. She set the tray next to him, grabbed some animal skins lying on the floor, and fluffed them as she laid them over his body. She looked him up and down, gently running her fingers through his hair and down his skull.

She had always pictured them larger than life as they killed the animals and destroyed the land. This man was nothing compared to her childhood visions, and sometimes, she thought he was cute. She had never seen a man up close and was told her entire life that they were monsters capable of terrible deeds. The things that went bump in the night, the shadows that lurked in the deepest recesses of their minds. She was taught that man was to be feared, not taken into their homes to be healed.

The man continued to shiver and relaxed, lying peacefully and calmly. *As peaceful as the devil could be,* she reminded herself, tucking the skins around his neck and laying her hands on his face, trying to feel the evil she knew lurked within.

"I don't know why Father has brought you here," she whispered, "But I hope for your sake he makes it."

Roa-ma moaned behind her. His arm was raised, and he mumbled something she couldn't understand. She hurried toward him, looking for his face, and rolled to her hands and knees. She grabbed his arm, pushed it onto the grass bed, and petted the top of his head.

"It's okay, Father," she whispered. "I'm here." She kissed his forehead and stretched back, grabbing the medicinal tray. Tears streamed down her cheeks as she removed the old dressing and looked at the wound. The medicine she applied earlier was still in place, and she prayed the bleeding had stopped.

The bullet entered through his right side, shattering his lowest two ribs and leaving a small hole. Shree had made an incision over the puncture, removed the damaged ribs, and sewn the edges together, making the tear as small as she could. She lifted his shoulder and rolled him on his side, exposing his back. The exiting bullet removed a chunk of his body below the shoulder, and the pink meat turned red with blood as she washed off the semi-dried mud.

The bullet had missed his vital organs, removing only muscle, but a piece of metal remained lodged in his body. Her fear of him bleeding to death kept her from removing it, and she hoped she was doing right. If he died, she would never be able to forgive herself. Tears swelled in her eyes, and she regained her composure. She rolled him on his back, petting the hair above his face and around his ears. She had never seen him hurt so bad.

She finished adding water and stirred her treatment, rolling him on his stomach. She filled the gaping wound with her remedy, pasting the wet leaves and plants over it. She sprinkled water and mud over them, gently patting them in place. "*Dear God, please don't let him die*," she prayed.

A dim light entered the room and diminished as Sah squeezed through the opening. "How are they doing?" he whispered.

She looked at him, wiping the tears from her face, and fell into his arms, crying.

He stroked the top of her head, holding it tight against his chest. "I've never seen him hurt so bad," she sobbed.

"Don't worry," he said, "Everything'll be all right." He felt the tears swell in his throat as she pulled away and turned her attention back to her father. He sat on the opening, eliminating the dim light emanating from the room above as she rolled him on his back, repeating the procedure on his abdomen. She dropped to the floor, crawling towards Sah, and sobbed as she lay her head in his lap. He stroked her head as she drifted to sleep.

Sah's chest heaved, and she purred as he caressed the hair on her face. He thought of Ahm and wished he was here. Father never allowed him to stay long, but he had been Shree's boyfriend for as long as he could remember. The older he got, the more he understood her yearning to be with him.

Their world was becoming smaller every year, and one territory couldn't support two families. A family passing without a sibling inheriting the land hadn't happened for centuries, and it was the only way they would ever be together. He thought of life with and without her and then of it without his father.

If he didn't pull through, the responsibility for both of them would fall on him. He wished Ahm could move in with them, and that he could be the one never to marry. The problem was that their bloodline was the oldest, and his ancestors were the ones spoken of in the scrolls. The council would never allow it.

Shree raised him after their mother died, and she was the most important person in his life. He would do anything for her, and thought trading places with her should happen. His father never spent time with him or taught him the keeper's ways.

He ran through the forest in his mind, doing his father's job. He had been following his father for a couple of years, but only recently was able to keep up with him. He knew there had to be more to this job than he had seen. He prayed it was a situation he wouldn't find himself in and that his father would be improving. He always expected he would be here with them forever and didn't like the idea of them being alone.

The results of his visions turned disastrous, forcing him back to reality. He needed more time. It was good he left the doe's when he did. He had a bad feeling and went to scan the perimeter of their territory after the animals were safely in the crown.

He heard his father's growling as he navigated the trees and headed towards it. He reached the clearing, seeing a man with a gun and smelling his father on the other side. He chattered like a squirrel, giving a warning. The growling subsided and stopped. Roa-Ma sprang from the trees as the gun exploded, and his father jerked backward, hitting the ground and disappearing into the trees. He raced around the clearing, finding a trail of blood, and followed it, watching his father collapse in the deep snow.

He panicked and fell to his knees, packing snow in his wounds. His father looked at him, demanding he capture the man, and Ahm suddenly appeared. Sah tried to comfort his father, but he persisted in capturing the man alive. He lay there barking out a plan. They set the trap as his father watched from a distance, calling on the animals to run through the field. He grabbed the little being, and Ahm cleaned up the mess before the animals arrived, wandering through the meadow, destroying the evidence of their existence. Sah helped his father to his feet and walked silently as the old man wheezed with every step.

He picked his sister's head from his lap, scooted from underneath it, and gently set it on the straw and grass. He crawled towards his father and watched his bloodied body raise the leaves on his chest in rhythm to his breath. He ran his finger under the leaves, lifted them, and looked at the wound. The blood slowed but hadn't stopped. If the bleeding stopped, he might stand a chance; if not, he would surely die. He crawled back to Shree, lying beside her, knowing she was the only one who could save him.

The man groaned. Sah's eyes snapped open, and he watched as the man mumbled incoherently. He crawled closer and rose to his knees, staring at the small figure. *He probably won't make it either*, he thought. *It would be better for us all if I killed him now and got it over with.*

He had developed his hatred for man just as his sister and his entire species had. They knew it would be man who would destroy them and take away their way of life. They also knew it was only a matter of time. Now, it seemed that his father had brought home the devil himself. Everything inside of him said it didn't belong here, and he had to do something about it. He looked at his sister, listened to the room, and slowly put his hand over John's nose and mouth, pressing down.

Shree opened her eyes and looked at him. "What are you doing?' She shrieked.

"Nothing, Shree, just looking at him," he nervously yelped, brushing the leaves and gently pushing some under the man's head.

"Looks like they aren't so evil after all, doesn't it?" she said, stretching and rolling to her father. Satisfied he was still breathing, she looked at Sah and headed towards the opening.

Yeah, he thought as she disappeared. "Not too evil at all." He followed her, making his way out of the room. *And if Dad's not up to answering some questions soon, we'll make sure this evil can't spread*, he thought, crawling through the passageway.

Shree was changing the bandages on her father's back as Sah looked for more medicinal roots, berries, and leaves. Her father gained some consciousness earlier that morning, and she had been tending to his unresponsive body since.

"Father," she asked with the man lying in his state of semi-consciousness on the other side of the room. "Why did you bring that man into our home?"

"I just have to find out..." came the surprising response as he drifted in and out of reality.

A sudden movement startled her, and the happiness she was feeling shattered. She dropped the tray she held, and it crashed on her father's chest. Roa-Ma cried out, drifting back to unconsciousness, and she watched as the man sat back down.

John sat, looking into the blackness surrounding him and seeing nothing. He rubbed his eyes, trying to adjust them to the dark, and pain shot through his body. *Where the hell am I?* he wondered.

A light twinkled through the foliage covering the opening ahead of him. He jumped to run as a branch broke before him, and an animal howled in pain. "Who's there?" he said as he sat back down, lowering his head. A hand reached out, touching him. He breathed a sigh of relief, feeling comforted by the contact, and grabbed the arm.

His yell resounded in the cave as his fingers touched the giant, hairy appendage. He instinctively bolted towards the opening, tearing the growth from it. The light grew stronger as he crawled closer to the top, and fresh air filled his lungs. He stepped into the large room that the tunnel emptied into, looking around.

A group of branches and leaves covered another opening he hoped led to his freedom. He ran for it and jumped, ripping away the growth. The light blinded him as he struck the ground, dropping the branches he carried. He squinted, regaining his sight, and ran as fast as his weak legs could move.

Sah, trying not to wander too far away while collecting the ingredients for his sister, heard the commotion coming from the cave and ran towards it. He arrived as the man crashed through their front door. It rolled through the deep snow, leaping from the ground and racing toward the trees.

Sah beat him to the heavy growth, tackling him in the cold, slushy ground. The man's head slammed on a rock, and he remained still as a small trickle of blood rolled down his neck.

"That's the last time I'm nice about this," Sah screamed as he picked him up like a rag doll and started back towards the cave. "Just give me one more reason, and I'll make sure you never live to make it back to the cave, no matter what Shree says."

II-VIII

Phil rolled the truck in front of its owner's home, turning off the key. It was four in the morning, and although he didn't know what to expect, it sure wasn't John's trailer sitting dark and silent.

He had driven all day and most of the night, and the thought of Sheila being in bed never crossed his mind. Now, he couldn't decide if he wanted to pry himself out of the truck and up the stairs. He closed his eyes and jerked himself from sleep.

What am I going to tell her? he thought, looking at the seat and running his hands through his hair. He wished he had a beer. John's disappearance was the only thing he'd been able to think about during his journey home, and he still hadn't decided on what to tell Sheila. What he did know was that he hadn't had a drink since yesterday, John was missing, and no one knew where he was or what had happened to him.

His head pounded, reminding him he needed to sleep soon. He burped, and the taste of rotten egg burned the back of his throat, reminding him of his heartburn and churning stomach. He rubbed his eyes, started the truck, and grinded the truck's gear into reverse. He would go home and sleep. Then, he could get his thoughts together and tell her when he was more prepared.

He revved the engine and slowly released the clutch as a light appeared in the window. "Great," he mumbled as he slammed the clutch to the floor, and the burning moved to the middle of his ribs. "*She must have heard the truck and thought it was John.*" He held his breath, allowing the pain to subside, and stared at the light, hoping it would turn off.

He wanted to leave but knew he had to tell her. He moved the gearshift into neutral and released the clutch. He turned off the key, pushed the emergency brake to the floor, and opened the door. *Maybe I'll be able to get some sleep when this is over*, he thought, picking the sand from his eyes and stretching his bent arms in the air. He slammed the door, looked at the lighted window, and walked towards the stairs.

He knocked on the door, and the porch light brightened his surroundings. Sheila appeared, her hair blowing in the frigid wind and her eyes trying to focus. She had obviously fallen asleep on the couch, drunk and passed out, while worrying about them not being home. Her beauty always enchanted him, and she was more stunning now than he could ever remember. His heart pounded at the sight of her, and he found himself stumbling for words.

"Well, why don't you guys let someone know when you're going to stay an extra day?" she slurred as he watched her walk to the couch and sit. "I've been sitting here for two days waiting for you."

The smell of alcohol lingered as he stepped in and closed the door. *Oh God, he thought, she's toasted*. He walked to the fridge, looked for a beer, and sat in the chair. He looked at her empty bottles and watched as she swayed, drifting in and out of consciousness.

"Where's John?" she questioned, suddenly realizing he didn't walk in.

"I don't know, Sheila; he went out early the other morning and never came back. I don't know what happened, he..."

"What do you mean you don't know what happened?" she snapped, looking like she was on the verge of becoming psychotic. "Are you telling me that you lost my husband?"

Oh dear God, he thought. This wasn't going the way he had played it over and over in his mind, and he was realizing this could have been one of the worst decisions he had ever made. "Well," he started, waiting for her to interrupt. "He left the other morning and never came back." He walked to the couch, waiting for her to respond. "I went looking for him and found his hat and some really weird tracks in the snow, but there were no signs of him."

Her demeanor lightened, and she looked at him, laughing at his joke, expecting John to walk through the door any second. "I get it." She smiled. "This is all a big joke. Come in, John, the joke's over, and it's not funny?"

"No, it's not a joke, Sheila." He took John's bloodstained hat and handed it to her. "The police will probably be here in the morning. That's why I drove all night—to get here first so I could be the one to tell you."

She jumped from the couch, ran out the door, and approached the edge of the deck, staring intently at the truck. Phil followed and stood next to her. "I'm sorry, Sheila, but I really don't know much else."

"Well, maybe we should start from the beginning," she stated soberly with a tear in her eye, still not believing his words. She turned and walked into the house with Phil shadowing her.

"Hey, Sarge, this could get interesting," Lieutenant MacDougal said, tapping the leg of the old timer sitting next to him. He repositioned himself, getting excited and trying to get a better look. "Come on, Sarge, what do you think?"

"It's possible," Sergeant Johnson replied, "but even if something goes on, it still doesn't prove anything. We don't have a body, and without a body, we don't have a case."

"Yeah, but if we find a body, this becomes his noose. We should take him in right now and give him the grilling of his life." He stared intently at the Sergeant, and silence filled the car. "You know, it's not like we're working on any real cases now anyway. We should hope to get lucky and make this guy confess to a murder." He smiled and tapped the Sergeant on the leg. "It sure couldn't hurt as a career move."

Johnson pulled the stub of a smoldering cigar from his mouth. "Yeah, I'd say we've got a pretty good handle on this town, and I doubt anything will come of this either. If you want action and a quick promotion, move to the city. If you need me, give me a nudge." He smashed the cigar butt in the ashtray and stretched back in his seat, placing his hat over his eyes.

He was growing increasingly irritated with the new recruits they kept teaming him with. Fresh out of the academy, and they knew it all. He spent twenty-two years on the force, and he was damn proud of his accomplishments. He felt he deserved better than these training assignments, and it was frustrating.

He was getting older, and his body wasn't all it used to be, but he missed the action. He couldn't get hurt if he stayed away from the action, but the thought of a big case excited him. Retirement was only a few years away, and he would do what he had always done— bite his tongue and do as he was told.

His adrenaline sped as he thought of this being the case to make him a name before he left. He closed his eyes, slowing his heart, and the thought faded into a ridiculous notion. *Maybe they'll offer me an early pension, and I can go where it's warm and the fishin's good*, he thought, breathing out and relaxing his body.

"I know it sounds weird, Sheila, but it's God's honest truth." Phil looked into her eyes as tears swelled and flowed down her cheeks.

"Why didn't you stay and look for him?"

He held back his urge to hold her. "I did, Sheila, and I didn't find anything. The police looked, search and rescue looked, everybody looked. In fact, they're still looking now. There wasn't anything more I could do except come back here and tell you what was going on."

"Nothing more to do?" Her voice cracked as the anger began to surface. "Nothing more to do? There was plenty more to do."

Her face turned red. "You left him out there to die like an animal."

Zach and Kirsten woke from the volume of her voice and began to cry. "Get me my coat, and I'll go find him myself." She stumbled and fell to the floor as she stepped towards the closet.

Phil jumped from the chair and grabbed her, picking her from the ground. She stood, steadying herself beside him. "You can't do this, Phil exclaimed. You'll never even find the place. And if you did, there would be nothing you could do."

"Don't you touch me, you bastard!" She yelled, pounding on his chest and twisting from his hold. Zach and Kirsten hysterically ran into the living room, standing next to their mother. "Get out! Get out of my house now!" She screamed, causing the children to cry louder. She leaned over, trying to console them, and picked her baby up, holding her in her arms. "You killed him!" She yelled.

He grabbed the door handle, trying to escape. The children screamed again, elevating his blood pressure and putting their mother into a frenzy. He fumbled with the lock on the doorknob, locking it and unlocking it. "I'm sorry, Sheila, I wouldn't..."

"Sorry? My husband is lying out there right now, dying because of you, and all you can say is you're sorry. Now get out of my house, you murderer!"

The door flung open, and he ran down the stairs, listening to her voice carry above the screams of the children. He reached John's truck and pulled open the door, jumping in. He slammed the clutch

127

to the floor and turned the key in the ignition, screeching down the road as he left.

"Hey, Sarge, I think you should watch this," MacDougal excitedly stated, nudging his partner.

Johnson pulled the hat from his face and sat looking at the trailer. "What happened?" he whispered.

"Nothing," his partner replied as Phil descended the stairs and jumped into the truck. "Just a lot of yelling and screaming so far."

"Women," Johnson mumbled, "Who can figure 'em?" The truck started and squealed down the road, skidding and regaining control. "Well, let this be a lesson to ya," the Sergeant said, pointing a finger at the newbie. "Nine times out of ten, these things are exactly as they appear. He grabbed his seatbelt and pulled it around him. "Stupid kid should have let us tell her in the first place. It's like I said, MacDougal, if you want action, move to the city." He buckled the belt in place. "Now let's go harass him about the way he left here, and then maybe we can go home and sleep."

The lieutenant looked at him in question. "But sir, shouldn't we stay here and make sure she's all right?"

"She'll be all right, MacDougal. Now let's go before we lose him."

MacDougal twisted the ignition and slammed the transmission into gear, spinning the tires and swerving. Johnson breathed deep and held his breath, bracing himself with his legs. MacDougal gained control of the powerful vehicle and sped down the road. "Are we going to arrest him and take him downtown to question him?" he asked, reaching for the siren.

Johnson grabbed his hand, stopping him from hitting the switch. "No. I think he's had enough excitement for one night. We're going to make him slow down, and we'll do it with just the lights on. Okay?"

He rearranged his body to get comfortable, leaned his head on the headrest, and watched as they approached the back of the truck.

II-IX

John's pupils dilated as his eyelids opened, and he tried to focus. Blackness surrounded him, and a nasty stench opened his nasal passages, souring his growling stomach. He coughed and put his hand in front of his face, slowly moving it towards him and tapping himself on the nose. *Oh my God, I'm blind*, he thought, hearing a movement on his right.

A cold rock dropped on his stomach, startling him. Footsteps scurried back to the other side of the room. They stopped, and a breath was exhaled. "Who's there?" he asked, waiting for a reply. His stomach growled as he put his hand on the stone plate. He felt slimy, icy pieces of something, and what felt like berries. His hand dropped into liquid, and he pulled it to his mouth, chugging it down.

He touched his tongue with his finger and slowly picked a handful of the lumpy slime, putting it in his mouth. It ran down the back of his throat as he swallowed, exhaling his approval. He lifted a root to his nose, smelled it, and put it in his mouth, snapping a small piece off. He slowly chewed the substance, tasting green and sweet. It wasn't a steak dinner, but it would keep him from starving.

Something else moved in the room, and a dull light shone, quickly returning to pitch black. *At least I'm not blind*, he thought, silently eating and trying to discern further movement.

He swallowed and grabbed another handful of the berries. He put them in his mouth and silently chewed, sucking the moisture from them. He flinched as the light reappeared, exposing a large figure approaching him. Fear overtook his weak, beaten body, diminishing all hope of escape. *What were they saving him for*? He thought, rolling into a ball and thinking of the stories and articles he had read about predatory animals.

Maybe they weren't animals at all, but a lost civilization of apes that had somehow remained hidden, he thought, as different scenarios of what was happening flashed through his mind. Images he had seen on television of cannibals carrying men hog-tied to a stick and forcing them into boiling pots of water popped into his mind. His face flushed, and his body tightened. He waited for some kind of event to happen.

Shree saw the man wake and decided to see his reaction before giving him the food she brought back the day before. She looked at her father, who had fallen back into a fever, and thought of him taking care of her through the years. She was young when her mother died, and she didn't remember much of her.

She touched her father's head and slowly petted his fur. She still wasn't sure why he had brought the man back, but during the last few days, he had drifted in and out of consciousness for a few minutes here and there, assuring her that there was a reason for it. He asked her to ensure nothing happened to the man before he got better, and he would explain it to them then.

She rolled him over on his stomach and pulled off the wet leaves to check and clean his wounds. The edges had started to scab over, but the center of the wound was still open and pink. Blood and bodily fluids were excreted from the hole, but they had slowed. The worry of him bleeding to death was no longer present. She soaked new leaves in the powder and water mixture, sitting next to her, and placed them over the wound.

Sah woke and crawled over to her as the dull light from the opening he was concealing reappeared in the room. "How's he doing?" he asked as he looked at the wound and then at her.

"It's looking better," she replied. It doesn't look infected, and if the fever breaks, he shouldn't have any more problems."

"And what about him?" He pointed towards John, who sat between him and the light.

"Oh, he'll make it," she stated, approaching nearer to the man. "Dad said he would tell us why he brought him here when he gets better." She leaned her head forward, trying to get a better look. "Kinda funny looking, don't you think?"

"Shree, stop, don't get so close." Sah nervously exclaimed, grabbing her and pulling her back.

John lowered his plate and set it on the ground, defeatedly. "More," he mumbled, "Please."

She looked at Sah and knelt down, grabbing the plate from the floor. She crawled through the small tunnel into the main cave, leaving Sah and the man alone. She grabbed more berries and water for him.

The room suddenly became dark again, and the large hairy hand set the plate back in front of him with the goblet of water next to the stone plate. Sah watched intently, waiting for the man to do something to his sister.

The man quickly drank the water and placed a handful of berries into his mouth, savoring the juices, knowing they would replenish his strength.

"I don't think he can do anything to me," she whispered as she passed her brother.

Shree sat beside her father, stroking his forehead and removing the sweat that continued to build there. His fever broke late last night, and he had been coming in and out of consciousness since. Sah hadn't left the room since the man regained his consciousness and kept an ever-watchful eye on him, hoping he would try to run or hurt his sister in some way.

The man had been sitting in the same spot since Sah brought him back to the cave. She wondered if he would ever move again. There were times she wondered whether he was dead or not, but his hands were always out when she came down with food. And he always wanted more.

She had been cleaning up his bodily functions from the beginning, but he had become stronger and more hostile during the last few days. The smell was horrible, and she knew it would become unbearable if she didn't have her brother take him out and clean him up while she cleaned the little sleeping area.

She wondered how they could live with such an awful stench as her father moaned and sat up. "Don't try to move," she insisted, pushing down on his shoulders and petting the fur on his head. She looked back at the man and focused her attention on her father.

John quietly sat and munched on some roots as he stared at the light coming through the small opening that led toward his freedom. He still had no idea what they planned to do to him, and he sure as hell didn't want to stick around to find out what it was. He had noticed steady breathing a few days ago and now knew why the constant commotion came from that area. He wondered if it was the one he shot.

Whoever it was, he was obviously held in high esteem. His eyes adjusted well enough to see a large mass of hair moving up and down, and he started making out the features of the other two entering and exiting the cave. He couldn't be positive about how they really looked and couldn't help but think about the dreams he was having before his trip. The resemblance of what he could remember and of what he had seen of these creatures scared him.

A low grumbling started where the hairy figure lay, and the ground began to rustle. He noticed his constant companion leave earlier, and the other quickly darted towards the noise. *This is my chance*, he thought. He was stronger now and knew he could make it. He slowly moved and then darted towards the dim light.

The light immediately vanished, and the room turned black as he ran into a large mass of flesh. It stepped backward from the impact and howled as it touched the hard, rough rock behind it. The figure's arm grabbed him and tossed him back into the corner of the room as if he were a rag doll. He crashed into the wall, almost breaking his shoulder, and crouched on the floor, waiting for the finishing blow.

His adrenaline pumped as the dim light reflected in his eyes. He thought about fighting his way to freedom and then about the pain in his shoulder. Whatever these things were, they were big and they were strong. There was no way he could get by all of them. *How many of them were there*? He didn't even know.

Shree grabbed her father to stop him from falling to the ground. "What are you doing?" she screamed, pushing him back on his bed of leaves. The dull light faded again and brightened as Sah appeared through the opening. "Don't be so stupid," she yelled. "Lie down, and don't you move again." She looked at Sah with an everything's all right look and rolled her father onto his stomach. "Sah can handle him, but you need to rest and not worry about it."

Sah breathed in and sat next to the opening. *That's it*, he thought. *The next time it moves, I'll kill it. No matter what anybody says.*

John opened his eyes and stretched his arms and legs. There was a lot of movement in the other corner of the room earlier, and it sounded like everybody had moved outside. He sat up and looked at the light coming through the large, round opening that led him out.

He stood and cautiously walked towards the light, pulling back the branches and growth. He figured it had been at least ten days since he arrived here, but had no idea of how long he had been asleep. He reached into the top pocket of his shirt and felt the cigarette pack still firmly in place. He had a tremendous urge to pull one out and light it, and wondered if he would ever have the chance to smoke again.

His thoughts turned to Sheila and the kids. He missed them, and the thought of never seeing them again brought a lump to his throat. He wondered if Phil came looking for him or if he was looking for him now. He wished he knew how long he had been here and where here was.

He put his hand to his chin and rubbed the stubble of his new beard. His rubbing turned to scratching, and he stuck his head in the opening, looking around, hearing and seeing nothing.

He thought he heard something move. He pulled back to his space and covered the opening. His ears perked up, and he heard only silence. He looked back at the dim light and slowly started up the narrow cave, hoping it would lead to his freedom.

Roa-Ma stood up, groaning loudly as Sah and Shree moved in to help if he fell. "Well," he started, "Once when I was a child, my father brought home a man he wounded in the forest. I became very intrigued with the man and would sit and pray he would wake up so I could talk to him and find out more about his race. I wanted to know if the stories we've heard all our lives were true." He hesitated momentarily and looked at Sah and Shree, who listened intently. "I wanted to know if it's possible to communicate and talk to them. I want to know if there's a way we can put aside our differences and live together in peace. Our race could depend on it."

He looked at the floor and then back at them as they sat silently. "Well, the man never woke up, and I never got to find out anything. We buried him not too far from where your mother lies." He sat silent for a moment. "When this man shot the buck I was tracking, I lost control and went crazy. The memories of your mother became so strong, and I charged him. He didn't intend to hurt me. He was just defending himself. When Sah knocked him out, I thought we could learn something from bringing him home. If nothing else, maybe he can help us learn enough about them so we can slow their killing and destructiveness."

"But Father," Sah interrupted, "What happens when this man returns to his world and tells his people about us?"

"I don't know," Roa-Ma responded, "We'll just have to face that when it happens." He breathed in deep, still cringing from the pain of his wound. "If we find out they are what we've been told they are, then we'll have to kill him. But until then, we'll keep him alive until we know."

John reached the end of the opening and slowly poked his head out, turning it in the direction where he knew the main entrance would be. A breaking branch startled him, and he instinctively twisted his head around to face the sound.

Roa-Ma was the first to hear the sounds of the man making his way through the tunnel. He stood and looked at the entrance of the sleeping room. Sah and Shree stood with him, hearing the soft scraping in the tunnel echoing into the large room. They followed their father's eyes to the entrance just in time to see the man's head poke out and look toward the exit.

Sah stood ready to capture him and do what he promised himself when his father motioned him to stay put. He picked up a large stick,

136

put it on the ground, and snapped it with his one good hand, getting the man's attention.

Father's looking better, Shree thought. It had been a couple of days since he got up, and it looked like he was starting to regain some of his strength. The wound stopped bleeding and had scabbed entirely, except for one small area directly where the bulk of the bullet had exited. She was tired of trying to keep the wet leaves on him while he was up and decided to let nature do the rest. She looked at the wound heaving in and out with his breathing as he snapped the stick. *I'll put more leaves on when he goes back to sleep*, she thought, *just to be safe.*

The man's head jerked around and looked at them. He froze and slowly sat next to the entrance, relinquishing all power as he looked at what had to be the leader holding the large end of the stick he had just broken. *God only knows how many more are outside*, he thought, sitting on the ground.

A low growl worked out of Roa-Ma's throat as he motioned the man to come and join them. John looked at the three things in front of him and cautiously watched as they watched him. He wondered if they were the big-foot creatures he read about in old folklore books or if they were a missing link to man. The older one's face was the being in his dream. He had leather-like skin surrounded his eyes, nose, and mouth. Gray and black hair surrounded the rest of his face, and he had a long beard flowing from his chin. John stared at them and made eye contact with Shree.

Those are Sheila's eyes, he thought as his heart slowed and a calmness overcame him. Her eyes were full of compassion and seemed as peaceful as his wife's the day he met her. She looked at him like a country child looking at a city zoo and feeling sorry for the caged animals.

137

He stood and slowly walked towards them. The large one, still standing, smiled and walked towards him. He pounded on his chest, trying to speak. "Roa-Ma," he growled, "Roa-Ma."

John formed a horrified expression on his face and turned to run. Roa-Ma's large hand reached out, grabbing and pulling him next to his chest, holding him there like a small child. John screamed, struggling and trying to get away. Roa-Ma gently stroked his head and held him tightly with the same arm. He hummed and started to purr. John's screaming slowly turned to sobbing as he fell to his knees. Roa-Ma patted his head and stroked him, pointing to the water rock. "Ah," Roa-Ma said as he pointed to the table. He put his hands to his mouth and imitated eating. "Eat," he growled.

John walked to the rock, sitting on the twigs and branches that surrounded it. Shree handed him a flat rock with roots and leaves on it. He looked at her again and gazed into her eyes. He couldn't get over how similar they were to his wife's. The beard the other two wore was absent, and he looked down at her small breasts and then back into her eyes.

Must be his daughter, he thought as he looked down, grabbing the roots and leaves.. *I wonder where his wife is*. He put one of the roots in his mouth and started eating when Roa-Ma looked at him and pointed to himself again. "Roa-Ma," he repeated. He looked over at the man with a puzzled look in his eyes and pointed at John, gently touching his shoulder.

"Ahh," he said, his voice rising in musical thirds. John looked into his eyes and thought of his wife and how many times she had given him that look. "Ahh," Roa-ma repeated again, pounding his chest and becoming irritated.

John sat up with a start. "What?" he said. "Oh, I see." He pointed back at the large figure. "Roa-Ma," he said. He then pointed back to himself and looked Roa-Ma in the eye again. "John," he said slowly. "John."

"AHN," Roa-Ma repeated, hitting him in the chest and laughing excitedly. "AHN," John smiled and looked at the other two who sat silently watching. He started feeling more comfortable and picked up another root from the plate beside him. He bit into it, and the strong taste of onion ran down the back of his throat. He spit it out, coughing and holding onto his throat. They laughed as Shree grabbed a rock cup full of water and handed it to him.

II-X

"Phil!" his mother yelled, banging on his bedroom door. "Phil, are you there?"

Phil pulled his blankets down past his head and looked at the door. "Yeah, I'm here!" he yelled, rolling over and closing his eyes."

"Well, don't you think it's about time you got up?" she screamed. "It's almost noon, and I think it's time you got yourself up. You're going to sleep your life away."

"Yeah, yeah!" he yelled over his shoulder. "Now, will you please leave me alone in here?" He had been out with some of his buddies all night and was in no mood for an argument.

"I just don't know," she started, "you kids today. I'm telling you, when I was your age, I certainly didn't sleep all day and stay out all night." She walked away frustrated. "As a matter of fact, I remember one time when..." she continued as she walked down the stairs and entered the kitchen.

Jesus, Phil thought as he rolled over on his back and stared at the ceiling. He had been back more than two weeks and still hadn't heard anything definite about John. He had called the police station several times and been put on hold or double-talked about the case being confidential. He thought they said they wanted to question him, but now they treated him like he didn't exist.

He rolled over and sat on the edge of his bed, grabbing his head with his hands and pulling his fingers through his hair. He could still hear his mother talking to herself as she slammed the cabinets shut, banging pots and pans, and preparing dinner for that night.

He rubbed the sleep from his eyes and walked to the mirror. He hadn't gotten much accomplished since John disappeared. His days were filled with sleep, while his nights were one long party. His normal six hours of sleep turned to twelve. He was depressed, and all of his attempts to cover it up weren't working.

He rubbed his bloodshot eyes and grabbed his housecoat from the floor. *I wonder if Sheila's in any better mood*, he thought as he slipped it over his shoulders. *"She should know if anything new has happened with the case."* He hadn't seen her since the night he told her about John. He thought about that night and every day since. I should call, he thought. John's a good friend, and I should make sure his wife and kids are okay until he gets back.

He unlocked his door and entered the hallway as his mother ran the vacuum cleaner. *That'll be the plan for the day.* He thought as he stepped into the hall and slipped into the bathroom.

He closed the refrigerator door and popped the top from the beer he took from the shelf. He walked to the table, picked up the sandwich he had just made, and took a bite. He walked to the phone, with adrenaline flowing through his veins from the thought of making the call.

That had been the pattern for the day. He would procrastinate until he had nothing else left to do, walk to the phone, think of something else, and then wander into a new adventure. He spotted a hairbrush lying on the breakfast bar and picked it up. He brushed out his hair and looked at the phone again. He sighed, picked up the receiver, and dialed with a shaky finger.

"Hello, Sheila," he nervously began, "This is Phil. How are you? Me? I'm pretty good...Yeah, I know that you were just upset... No, that's okay... No really. Listen, the reason I was calling was to see if you had heard anything about John. No...? Nothing...? Yeah...well, are you and the kids doing okay? Good. Is there anything that I can do for you? Anything you need?" He smiled as she spoke and looked over at the clock. "Sure, I'll be there in a few minutes." He hung up the receiver and walked towards the front door, taking another bite of his sandwich and pulling the car keys from his pocket.

"We're doing all right," Sheila said sobbingly. "I really just needed someone to talk to over the age of five." Her face contorted. "Do you know what I mean?' She burst into tears and dropped her head into her hands.

"Hey, I understand," he said softly. He sat silent, not knowing what to say or do, and started to tap his foot. Sheila sniffed and somewhat regained herself as she looked back at Phil and tried to smile. The black rings under her eyes looked like she had been in a fight, and she hadn't done her hair in days. He doubted if she had been out of her bathrobe since he told her of John's disappearance.

He felt compassion and wanted to hug her, but he felt uncomfortable and began nervously shifting in his chair, looking around the room. He wondered if her hair had been cleaned since John disappeared. "It must be hard on you," he blurted out. "With the children and all, I mean." She looked at him and tried to smile again.

"It's been hard on you, too," she replied. "I mean, after all, you were there when it happened." She started crying again.

He stepped to her and put his arms around her. "It's okay," he said. "John's out there somewhere. I know he is."

She pulled away from him and looked in his eyes. "I don't think so," she sobbed. "Something's happened to him. I just know that something's happened to him. I can feel it."

"Come on now," Phil whispered, holding her again. "He'll turn up soon." He rocked her back and forth and kissed her on the top of her head. "Where's Kirsten and Zach?"

"Zach should be home from school pretty soon, and Kirsten's in my room taking a nap."

"Oh, okay. Then why don't you go lie down for a while, and I'll make us all something to eat." He took his arms from around her neck and wrapped one around her waist, walking her through the kitchen and towards her bedroom.

"You really don't have to do this," she half heartedly argued.

"I insist," Phil rebutted. "Now get back in there and get some sleep." He waited for her to close the door and walked to the kitchen cabinets. *What the hell did I get myself into this time,* he thought. *I don't even know how to cook.*

He paced to the refrigerator and opened it to find a carton of milk, a jug of Kool-Aid, a jar of Jelly, and some mayonnaise. He closed the door and plopped down at the kitchen table.

Zach burst through the door and stared at Phil. "Hi," Phil said, smiling and waving as he stood there staring at him.

"What are you doing here?" Zach asked in a very motherly voice. "And where did you put my mom?" He folded his arms and tapped his foot on the ground, looking Phil in the eye and waiting for an answer.

Where did he learn this? Phil thought as he stepped back and viewed the situation. "She's all right, you know," he said like a spoiled child. Zach persisted in tapping his foot. "She's in the bedroom lying down with your sister," he finally said, exasperated and throwing his hands in the air.

Zach ran to the bedroom and slammed the door behind him. Kirsten started to cry from the noise and was quieted by her mother. Phil put his hands on his sides and waited for Zach to return.

He ran to Phil and looked up at him. "Okay," he said. "My mom said it was okay for you to be here and that you're gonna fix us something to eat."

"Um, yeah, that just about sums it up, I'd say," Phil replied. "But it seems that the only thing to eat around here is..."

Peanut butter and Jelly," Zach finished. "Can we please get a pizza. Please?" he emphasized as he looked at Phil with sad eyes.

"Now that's a great idea," Phil exclaimed, snapping his finger. "And while we're waiting, I can run out and grab us some beer. Great idea, little dude."

"Yippee!" Zach screamed as Phil walked to the telephone and started to dial.

Kirsten's body went limp, and she stopped crying as Phil paced through the trailer with her in his arms. "Oh, thank you, God," he said quietly, not to wake her again.

He had been walking and bouncing the infant for what seemed like a lifetime and thought she would never stop crying. He walked into the kids' room, placed her in the crib, and was almost out the door when she started to cry again.

He returned to the crib and picked her up, lightly bouncing her in his arms. He heaved out his breath in frustration and walked back into the living room, bouncing Kirsten once again.

Sheila emerged from the hallway and entered the kitchen. She looked at Phil and smiled, putting her arms out for her baby. "I'm sorry to be such a nuisance," she said. "Here, let me have her." Phil handed over Kirsten's again limp and quiet body to Sheila. "This time, I think she's out for the night," Sheila stated as she walked into the bedroom and carefully put her in her crib. Phil walked to the couch and sat down. He ran his fingers through his hair and rested his head on his hand. Sheila came out of the bedroom and sat down next to him.

"I'm sorry," She said, sitting down and touching his leg with her hand.

He looked up at her, startled. Her sky-blue eyes sparkled in the dim light of the room. He stood up, nervously put his hands in his pockets, and walked towards the door.

"Are you sure you wouldn't like a cup of coffee or something?" she asked innocently.

"Yeah, I'm sure," he said, looking at his watch. "It's getting late, and I need to get home." He picked up his coat and headed for the door. "Bye."

She walked to him and kissed him on the cheek before he could escape. "Thank you," she said. "You've really been a big help." He put his arms around her and squeezed her tight. Her warm, small-framed body felt good against his, and he didn't want to let go.

"I'll stop by tomorrow," he said, "and if you need anything until then, just give me a call." He let go of his grip, walked out the door, and headed toward his car.

Wow, he thought as he unlocked his car door. *What a beautiful woman she is. John is sure a lucky man.* He opened the door and got in. A smile overtook his face as he celebrated his perceived victory. He started his car, pulled out of the driveway, and drove off into the start of what had already become a beautiful day.

II-XI

John stepped outside and breathed in as a flock of geese flew in formation overhead. He watched as they honked and faded into the clouds. *Must be some kind of procrastination ducks*, he thought as he looked around the forest and then back into the sky.

Sah appeared from behind a tree and froze, staring at him. He held up his hand to wave, and his new friend disappeared as quickly as he had appeared. John looked back at the cave's covered opening and then back at the trees. Roa-Ma had gone to bed a few minutes ago, and John stepped outside in anticipation of smoking before joining him.

He felt around his top pockets and pulled out a cigarette. He looked at it in contemplation for a few moments, thinking that he should just quit. He dug out his lighter and looked around for Sah, contemplating whether to throw it down. He placed it into his mouth and looked around again. *Looks like I could be here for a while*, he thought as the flame reached the tip of his cigarette, and he breathed in. The smoke fogged out of his mouth as he cupped the smoking stick, trying not to be conspicuous.

He became light-headed and dizzy as he thought about how long it had been since he tasted tobacco. He looked at the stars and then back into the forest as his legs grew weak from the initial jolt of nicotine. He had no idea where he was or if he could escape these things. He knew he could get lost in the woods and be dead before finding any form of civilization. Winter settled in, and he knew if he didn't make his move soon, he would be here until spring.

A twig snapped in the distance, and a wolf's howl echoed in the sky. He scanned the trees again and walked closer to the cave entrance. It was apparent they weren't going to kill him. At least not right away. Sah was his constant companion, but he had felt no aggression.

They spent the last few days trying to communicate. They attempted to communicate through a very basic form of body language, with most of the communication occurring through a series of grunts and body movements. All John had been able to make out were a few essential words, such as eat, sleep, drink, plate, and cup. He felt it was impossible to teach them his language, and with the mounting frustrations after each day of failure, he didn't want to stick around to see what was going to happen next.

He looked at the top of the cave and peeped through a small opening in the trees. A light flashed for an instant and was gone. *What was that*? He thought as he walked towards it. He thought about his family and what they would be doing now. "*Dear God, please let me get out of this alive, and I swear that I will never kill anything again,*" he vowed as the exhaled smoke from his cigarette engulfed his head. He smashed the cigarette onto the ground. He stomped on it, twisting his foot in the ground, making sure it was extinguished, and walked towards what he hoped would only be his temporary home.

John panted and gasped for breath as he reached the top of the hill and the end of the trees. A sheer rock cliff overcame him, and he stepped back, sinking into the deep snow. A rock towered two hundred feet into the air, forming a semicircle and covering the top of the mountain he was on. Snow-capped the peak, and it was indented by the small crevasses and cracks that followed it up.

Five minor points extended upward, perfectly spaced apart, and precisely the same height. The full moon sat against them and lit up the sky, making the formation look like a giant, glimmering crown.

Sah walked up from behind and stood beside him while John obliviously stared at the rock, unaware of Sah's presence. *"Crown of the Keepers"* came to John's mind as he looked at Sah and stepped back into the deep snow, startled. He stumbled and fell onto his back as Sah quickly vanished into the trees.

He sat in the snow, staring at the stars, feeling drained and tired. Galaxies of stars blinked from the sky. He had never seen so many stars. He stood up and brushed the snow from his clothes. *Must be getting late*, he thought, wondering if it was Sah who had told him the name of the rock he was looking at earlier. He shook his head and slowly started back towards the cave.

Roa-Ma opened his eyes and sat up. He held his breath and slowly stood, fighting the pain. The morning was the worst, and waking up always made him remember how badly he was hurt. He had been sleeping for a while, and the scab that covered his wound cracked with his every movement.

It's getting better, he thought, and although he still had no feeling in three of his fingers and part of his arm, he hoped that in a couple of weeks, he'd be healed and back to his ways. He walked to the man sleeping on the twigs and leaves where Sah and Shree usually slept. He looked at him, silently sleeping, and sighed.

He had always dreamed of having a man he could talk to and teach about the outside world. But now that he had him, it was becoming evident that communication would be impossible. He knew that unless something happened soon, the man would have to die.

All of his childhood dreams were shattered, and this was possibly the biggest mistake he had ever made. It was just as they had always been taught. Humans were nothing more than destruction sent from hell to destroy all the beauty either of them had ever known.

If he got back to his people and told them about his family, it could launch an attack. The written words would begin and would start the slaughter of his race throughout the world. It was written that they would not survive. He walked towards the dim light and crawled into the opening towards the dawn of a new day.

A large stick popped from the pressure of a large animal stepping on it behind him. John turned, expecting to see his companion, and looked into the eyes of a mountain lion instead. It looked at him and yawned, licking its lips and showing its teeth. John looked for an exit, knowing what was coming, and screamed. He desperately ran. The lion hesitated and crouched down, springing and chasing after him.

Roa-Ma stepped in front of John, taking the cat's blow. He stepped back, grabbed the intruder by the neck, and slammed it into a tree. He growled and threw his arm in the air, warning it to back off.

The lion wiggled up from its back and painfully lifted its muzzle towards Roa-Ma like a house cat being punished. It looked at John one last time and trotted away, angry that he wouldn't have a leisurely dinner tonight.

Roa-Ma turned around and looked at John. *What a stupid thing to do,* he thought. *That lion could have done the job for me.* Sah told him about the man breathing smoke and fire, and he wondered if he would ever learn anything from him. The man hadn't shown any

149

hostilities yet, so he thought he would give him a little more time before eliminating him forever.

He looked at John's horrified face and began to laugh. He hit him in the shoulder and fondly pointed towards the cave. John looked at him, wondering how he could thank him. They were a strange breed of animal. They were organized and had a way of communicating, but how they did so baffled him. The few grunts and signs they made still didn't leave him with much more than their names and some essential words. He looked at Roa-Ma's face and laughed a fake laugh as he looked at his eye-level chest. They turned and walked towards the cave.

They reached an unobstructed clearing that seemed to last forever. John had never seen this mountain range before and knew he could be hundreds of miles from anything. Any search would have been called off by now, and he knew he was on his own to get back to his family.

He wondered how his family was doing without him and if they thought he was dead. He missed them and thought that if he saw them again, it would be by freak chance. If they were going to kill him, he wished they would do it and get it over with.

He looked at Roa-Ma and then at the trail in front of him. Something wasn't right. They had been walking for at least half the day, and this didn't look like the way back to the cave. They continued through the trees when they entered a clearing, and Roa-Ma stopped. They cautiously walked into it, and John could see where the two mountain ranges came together, forming a U shape in the far distance, framing a large snowcapped peak. Two enormous cliffs jutted down the sides in front of them, and a rounded rock resembling a face sat to one side. *Oh my God,* John thought, *this is the place.* He sat down in the cold, wet snow, putting his head in his

150

hands and visualizing where his father had made him shoot his first deer above the rocky cliffs.

Seeing that John was no longer behind him, Roa-Ma turned around and retraced his tracks. *Now what*? He thought as he found the man sitting in the snow.

This is the place where my father forced me to kill my first deer. John's subconscious mind answered back.

Roa-Ma stepped back, astounded, and looked at him. *He answered me*, he thought excitedly. "*What did you say*?" he asked.

John looked at him and then back at the range, hearing nothing. Roa-Ma hurried him back towards the cave. "Sah, Shree!" he yelled with excitement. "I think the time's right for Sah's ritual of manhood."

Sah looked at him with a smile as he walked through the door. "Spring is almost here, son, and I think it's time you become a man." Sah stood silent, smiling, overcome with excitement, and not knowing what to say. "If I have this figured right, I should be able to induce a conversation with the man simultaneously," Roa-Ma mumbled as he walked towards the back of the cave.

Sah looked to the ground. The smile disappeared from his face, and his resentment of the man was building. "Putting me on the same level as a man?" He mumbled, showing his disappointment. He wondered if his father would still want the ritual if this man wasn't around. "Why does the man get to be in my rites?" he asked. His father looked at him, caught up in his thoughts and not hearing a word. He looked at John with a look of disgust and turned, angrily walking out of the cave.

151

II-XII

Phil walked up the wobbly stairs and stood with his heart pounding. He breathed deeply, slowing his heart, and knocked on the door. He stood for a moment and banged on the door harder. A few minutes passed, and he heard the door unlock. Sheila slowly opened the door and looked at him through the chain connecting the door and the wall. "So, what do ya need?" she asked, not moving.

He looked at her in her robe. Her hair was messy, and her eyes looked like she had been crying all night. "Oh, nothing, I umm...was just in the neighborhood and thought I'd stop by." He smiled and pulled a bouquet of flowers from behind his back. "And here, umm...I found these on the side of the road and thought about you. Can you imagine someone throwing them on the side of the road like that?"

She looked at the flowers, unlocked the chain, and turned around, walking to the couch and sitting down. She watched Phil walk in and close the door behind him. She ran her fingers through her hair and pulled it back, sighing while not taking her eyes from him.

Phil threw the flowers next to the empty wine bottles on the ottoman and sat in the chair beside the couch. "Rough night last night, huh?"

"Yeah," she whispered as she stood and walked into the kitchen. "You want something to drink?"

"Um, no," he said, jumping up and following her into the kitchen. He leaned against the counter as he watched her pour a cup of coffee and pull down a bottle of vodka from the cabinet. "Have I done something to upset you?"

"No."

"Then is something wrong?"

"No."

"Well, all right," he mumbled as he returned to the couch.

Sheila poured the liquid from the bottle into her cup. "You know, I've been thinking, and I don't know how you're doing for money, but it's been almost four months since John's been missing, and I've had people talking to me about some work." She turned around and looked at him as she gulped the alcohol from her cup. "And, well... I think if we teamed up using John's general contractor's license, we could both make some money."

Her ears perked up, and she looked at him as if he had lifted a weight from her. "You know, a really good band is playing at the Steer tonight, and my mom has the kids this weekend." He looked at her. "Why don't you come back and get me a little later? We can talk about it more then." She smiled at him and walked to the television, turning it on and joining him on the couch.

The band's volume was deafening as they walked into the small club, glancing around and looking for anybody they knew. "What do you want to drink?" Phil yelled in Sheila's ear as he looked at the bar and checked out the waitresses who crowded around it.

"Margarita," he read off her lips and headed towards the bar. She watched him until he reached the bar and scanned the room for a vacant table. She spotted one and walked towards it while watching the band.

"Thank you, and let's not forget about those waitresses and bartenders. The singer announced. They're working hard for you, so show them some appreciation. We'll be back right after this short break." The drummer stood from his throne. The guitar and bass players took the straps from their instruments and set them in their waiting stands. They smiled, looking over the crowd, and walked off the stage.

"So, what do you think about my offer?" Phil asked, setting down his beer and looking around for one of the waitresses.

She took a drag off her cigarette and blew out the smoke. "I don't know, Phil. What would I have to do?"

"Well, about the only thing I can't do is take care of the books." He looked into her eyes with other thoughts in mind, spotting a waitress and waving at her. He caught her attention and looked back at Sheila.

The waitress approached and looked at Phil. "Another beer and margarita?" He smiled, looking her in the eye, nodding, and checking her out as she wrote down the order.

"And two shots of tequila," Sheila blurted out, smiling and looking at Phil as the waitress acknowledged her order and walked off. "Okay, I can do it." She laughed. "I mean, I can take care of the books for you." She looked around at the crowd as the band walked on stage and began tuning their guitars. "Now, let's have some fun and not worry about any more business tonight. Okay?"

The waitress walked to their table and set their drinks down as Phil dug in his pocket, pulled out some money, and threw it on the tray. "Keep the change and make sure we don't go dry," he winked.

She looked at the money lying in her tray and then back at Phil. "Thank you," she smiled seductively. She looked at Sheila with a snotty look and walked away.

Sheila picked up one of the shot glasses and held it in the air. "Cheers," she exclaimed as Phil raised his glass and tapped hers on the side. She threw the alcohol in her mouth and swallowed as she picked up her beer to chase the burn.

"Why don't you come in for a little while?" she asked as they sat in his running car. She looked up at her small home. "I've got some beer in the fridge, and the night's still young," she slurred and giggled as she looked at him. "So, what do you say?"

"Well, okay," he muttered as his surroundings started spinning. He wondered how he had driven this far. "But we really shouldn't have done those last two shots." He laughed and opened his door, staggering into the cold night air.

"I'm telling you, Sheila, I really feel good about putting this business back together and..." He belched and looked over at her. "Oh, excuse me." He smiled. "But anyway, with the number of people that I've been out talking to lately, I really think we can both make enough money so we can live and not have to worry about paying our bills ever again." He grabbed his beer and guzzled some more, wondering why he was drinking more.

"God knows I could use that right now," she slurred. Their eyes met, and a silence engulfed the room.

"Have I ever told you how absolutely stunningly beautiful I think you are?" he asked, laughing and wishing he hadn't.

She walked to him and pressed her pelvic area into his. She placed her arms around his neck and softly kissed him on the lips.

He looked at her, stunned, and placed his hand behind her neck, pulling her closer and passionately kissing her. He slowly closed his eyes, and his surroundings began spinning again. He quickly opened them, but the room continued going around in circles, making him sick. He grabbed Sheila by the shoulders and pushed her back while looking into her deep blue eyes, feeling his stomach enter his throat.

"I'm sorry," he slurred, but I'm really not feeling very good right now. Those last couple of shots really got me, and I..." He raced towards the bathroom, heaving the excess alcohol from his system as he dropped to his knees, hugging the porcelain throne, not wanting to let go.

Phil pulled back the window curtain and peered out as Zach and Kirsten jumped out of their grandparents' car. He wiped his hands on the towel hanging from the refrigerator door and glanced at the small portion of food cooking in the pan. He tossed the towel on the counter and walked to the front door. He opened it and stepped outside onto the porch, waiting for them.

He passed out on the bathroom floor last night, and when he woke the first time, Sheila was in bed, and he carried himself to the couch. Now, he had been awake for almost two hours, had a pounding headache, and had started cooking a few minutes earlier in anticipation of her waking.

Her mother, an older woman with Sheila's blue eyes and deep wrinkles, walked up the stairs and handed Kirsten to him as Zach ran up behind them. "Is Sheila here?" she asked.

"No, she uh...she wasn't feeling well, so she's still in bed, but it's about time for her to wake up. If you'd like to come in and wait, I can go wake her for you." He looked at her, smiling and moving from the doorway, inviting her in. It was easy to see where Sheila got her looks.

"Oh, no, thank you. Henry's in the car waiting for me. We have a party for his boss we have to go to, and we're not even dressed yet." Kirsten lay her head on Phil's shoulder and closed her eyes. "I did want to thank you for helping her out during these bad times that she's having. I just don't know what she would be doing without you. She's really needed to get out of this house and have someone help her with these kids for a long time."

Her wrinkles deepened as she smiled, and her intense beauty shone through her rough face. She reached up and kissed him on the cheek. "You're such a nice boy," she said as she turned around and started walking down the stairs. "Tell Sheila I'll just give her a call later tonight. Okay?"

"I will," he replied, "and thank you." He watched her get in the car and shut the door. He turned, walked back into the trailer, and closed the door as the old vehicle rumbled down the road.

He looked at Zach, who was sitting on the couch with a cookie in his hand. "What's for lunch?" he asked.

"Fried chicken and eggs," he replied, laying Kirsten next to her brother. She sighed, rolling onto her back and sprawling out. She kicked her brother, who watched Phil walk into the kitchen. He jumped up, turned on the television, and returned to the couch. Phil pulled down some flour from the cabinet and opened the fridge, grabbing the remaining chicken and eggs.

He took the cooked pieces of chicken from the pan and placed them on a paper towel. As he watched television, Zach silently stared from the living room couch, arms crossed and a stern look on his face. He glanced at Phil. "Why don't you give me a hand and set the table?" Phil asked as he took plates out of another cabinet and placed them on the table.

Sheila opened the door to her bedroom and walked to the kitchen. Zach dropped the plates on the table and ran to her with his arms open wide. "Mommy!" he yelled as she bent down, picking him up and carrying him in one arm. She stepped into the kitchen, looked at Phil, who was busy over the stove, and set him down. "How are you feeling?" she asked, walking by him.

"Pretty good," he replied, "Everything's about ready and all at the same time, too. I must be getting domesticated." He laughed. "Did you sleep good?"

157

"Oh yeah," she answered, still glowing. She walked by him, intentionally rubbing herself against him as she passed. She picked up the plates and finished the task Zachary had started.

"Wow, this is delicious," she announced as she put the partially eaten thigh on her plate.

"Thanks," Phil gleamed back. "It's an old family recipe."

Kirsten knocked her glass over, spilling milk on the floor. "Kirsten Ann!" she yelled as she jumped up and grabbed a towel from the refrigerator door handle. She threw it on the spill, picked up the glass from the table, and cleaned the milk from under it. "Now, you be more careful next time." She looked at Phil seductively, smiling. "So what are we doing tonight?"

"Oh, I don't know, I thought that maybe we could watch some tube and hang out. I need to get out of here early tomorrow. It's time to get back to work." He winked at her, checking out her body for the thousandth time, and thought about what would have happened if he hadn't been so drunk. He had always wanted her and thought she was, without a doubt, the most beautiful woman he had ever seen. He mentally kicked himself and smiled seductively back at her.

"Sounds good to me," she responded. "It's a school night anyway, so these guys need to take baths and get to bed early. They've had such a busy weekend."

"Here we go," Phil said as he came through the door and looked at Sheila, who was cleaning up the mess he had made earlier. He walked to the fridge and put a twelve-pack of beer and a bottle of wine he purchased inside."

"What did you get?"

"I don't know the cheapest stuff they had." He laughed as he grabbed a glass from the cabinet and a beer from the refrigerator. He unscrewed the top of the wine bottle and poured it into the glass. He walked into the living room, sat on the couch beside her, and handed her the glass.

"So, what do you think happened to John?" he asked, not thinking and trying to make small talk. Sheila looked at him with a surprised look on her face. It wasn't a subject either one of them had brought up in a while, and she hadn't planned it would be brought up again. "I mean, come on, it's been four months?"

"I don't know." She became solemn and looked at the floor.

"I'm sorry, Sheila; I thought that maybe we were at a point where we could talk about this."

"He's dead," she mumbled through her tears and gasps.

"What?"

"I just know he's not coming back, Phil." She looked at him with a lump in her throat and began crying. "I can feel it."

Phil looked at her and clumsily put his arms around her. "Shhh..." He hugged her, trying to rock her. "He'll be back. You just wait and see." He knew John was dead, too, but he never wanted to let her know he thought that. Nobody could survive a harsh winter in the mountains alone. And unless he intentionally set the whole thing up to get out of whatever he was in, he had to be dead.

Sheila pulled away and looked at him. They stared at each other silently for a moment, and Phil stretched over, gently kissing her lips. "I'm sorry," he mumbled as thoughts of John walking through the door raced through his mind. He quickly pulled away, looking at her mouth and eyes.

He melted as she returned his advances, and they kissed again, longer and harder. His pants tightened, and his hands wandered over her breasts and body. She pulled away and looked at him, moving the hair from his mouth. "Let's go in the bedroom," she whispered, "It's much more comfortable in there."

Phil became lost in passion and began kissing her again. She slowly pulled away again and stood up with him, following her as far as he could with his lips. "Come on," she whispered. She grabbed him by the shirt and pulled him up, kissing his neck and leading him back to her bed.

II-XIII

Shree lifted her head, smelling for danger. She ran up the hill they were on as John tried desperately to keep up with her. He gave up and started walking, knowing she wouldn't let him get too far behind. The past several days had become busy around the cave. The snow was melting, and the warmth was a welcome change.

Roa-Ma returned from the journey he had left on a week earlier, and it seemed to John that they started preparing for somebody's arrival after he left. He bent over, supporting himself with his hands resting on his knees and his lungs burning with each breath he took. They had been running since early this morning. *This could be the cruelest way to kill someone ever.* He thought.

She stopped at the top of the ridge they were on and watched as the man leaned over, holding himself on his bent knees and breathing hard. She looked out over the valley and noticed movement out of the corner of her eye. She froze and dropped as she focused her gaze on the area.

A deer was twisted in a barbed wire fence, hanging upside down and kicking its hind legs in the air, trying desperately to escape. Each movement cut another hole into its skin, and blood ran to the ground. Wire fences and man's waste were some of a deer's greatest dangers. A new fence was one of the most dangerous, and this fence wasn't there the last time Shree ran on this trail. They are starting to get so close, she thought as she lifted her hand to her mouth and started running down the hill toward the animal.

She reached the deer and stopped as John made it up the side of the ridge, noticing why she was in such a hurry.

She put one hand to its snout, allowing it to smell it, and stroked its neck with the other. It was a large buck with three branches of antlers on each horn. The spring started to bring the velvet to its horns, and the blood-stained snow underneath was evidence that he had been struggling for quite some time. She doubted it would live long enough for her to apply her medicines and nurse him back to health.

She started purring, and the deer became calm, turning its head and looking at John. His large brown eyes filled with fear and slowly turned to death. She gently held the animal in one arm while trying to untangle it from the fence. Its blood continued to feed the red pool that lay beneath him.

John stared at the animal's body and then at its eyes. The body twitched as she freed the barbs from its raw flesh. He thought about how much meat would go to waste and how badly his family would need it by now.

She freed the animal and picked it up, carrying it away from the fence. She sat down with its head lying in her lap and began to sob. Its tongue extended from its mouth, dripping blood on the white snow as she rocked it back and forth. "*I have to do something to help*," he heard her say as she grabbed the leather pouch on her side.

He stood hypnotized by the deer's eyes as they slowly glossed over. It twitched again with a force that made Shree hold on as if she were riding a bull. She sobbed uncontrollably as the deer became still and twitched one last time. They watched as life exited from its body. She looked at John gently, setting the deer's head on the ground and standing. He could see the tears running down her face as she looked at him with a cold glare.

"There...there was nothing I could do," he yelled. "I didn't do it."

She turned her head, bent down, and started digging. He watched for a moment, figuring out what she was doing, and sighed. He walked over and kneeled down, helping her. She smiled as if to apologize, and they both continued digging the animal's grave.

They finished covering the body with dirt and stood. He looked at the tips of the antlers sticking out of the loose ground while Shree jumped up and down on the dirt. John kneeled, pushing dirt into the dents her packing was leaving, and smoothed the ground with his hands.

John's beard was wet from his sweat as he sat down and looked at Shree. Blood stained the fur on her chest, stomach, and legs. He stroked the damp hair on his face and looked into the setting sun, wondering what he looked like with a beard. She lifted her hand. "Come," she said with a husky animal growl, motioning him forward. He stood breathing in deep, getting ready for the run. She began running at a slow gallop, and John started after her, turning his slow walk into a sprint.

He reached the top of the mountain, where Shree patiently waited. He sat down, grabbing the pain in his side as he heaved in and out. He rolled onto his stomach and back, trying to catch his breath, and looked at the sky.

Shree looked at him and began laughing at the sight of him rolling around on the ground. *How funny these creatures are*, she thought. They're nothing like the monsters she had pictured in her mind.

John stood still, trying to catch his breath. "Yeah, you think this is funny, don't you?" he stated, looking at Shree, knowing he amused her. He looked over the horizon and leaned back, still holding his side. He slowly lifted his head and looked back out over the valley. He double-took a large dirt area with yellow graders dotting the hole they cut into the side of the mountain. He stood up, arching his back while being able to breathe again, trying not to show his excitement.

He looked at Shree and tripped as he started running down the hill. He slid down the hill fifteen feet, falling to his back. He picked himself up and started running again. *They could use a little grace*, she thought as she watched and began loping behind him.

With his heart pounding from excitement, John stopped and looked at the mining area standing almost a hundred yards before him. Shree passed him and continued towards the site. Something was wrong. None of the bulldozers were moving, and there wasn't any movement in the area. *Maybe it was lunchtime*. He hoped as he continued inspecting the barren and rugged site.

He reached the edge of the field and stopped, looking around. *No cars, no people, no nothing*, he thought, looking at the road winding through the mountain in front of him. "Oh crap," he said aloud, sitting down on the track of a backhoe. It had to be Sunday.

Shree came up from behind him, pulled him to her breast, and stroked his head. John pulled away from her and ran, jumping on one of the bulldozer's tracks and climbing onto the seat. He looked at the empty ignition switch and jumped down, running to the next one and then to the third. He hit the third one out of anger. No keys. He looked at Shree, watching him, and jumped to the ground.

"Why did you bring me here?" he yelled. Shree didn't move. "Why did you bring me here?" He looked back at the bulldozer he had just jumped from and walked to the back of it. He opened the metal pane, exposing the battery and motor, and searched for a moment, grabbing two wires.

Shree wandered behind him and watched as he touched the two wires together, creating a spark. She grabbed his arm and jerked him around, running off into the forest, carrying him as she went. He

164

struggled for a minute, knowing she wouldn't let him near the dozers again, and gave up.

She sat him down and looked into his eyes. She grabbed his hands, turned them over, and looked at his palms. Blood dripped down the fresh gash of opened meat on his hand. *It had to have happened when she was pulling him away from the machines*, she thought as she pulled some herbs and leaves from her concealed leather satchel and put them over the cut.

She pressed tightly on his hand, trying to stop the bleeding. She wandered around looking for a plant with a long root or a vine she could pull out of the ground and wrap around the cut. The leaves and herbs would never stay in place if she couldn't find one.

She reached the edge of the clearing they came from and took her eyes off of him. She looked down and picked up an old, brittle bird's nest. She looked at it for a moment, touching whatever was inside, and then held it out, placing it in his hands. He looked at it and then back at her with a quizzical expression on his face. "I don't understand," he said, shrugging his shoulders.

She pushed the nest back at him, making the sound of a chirping bird. He looked at her again and shook his head no. She stood up, frustrated, and grabbed the tree branch beside her. The large branch cracked as it fell towards the ground, and another nest fell on her head. It broke into pieces and fell to the ground. John saw what she was trying to show him. Three newborn birds looked up, their mouths open wide and their wings extended. Parts of their shells stuck to the various nest materials and surrounded their dead, decaying bodies.

My God, he thought. *They died soon after coming out of their shells.* He looked toward the bulldozers and then up at the sky through the treetops. The sky's bright blue silhouetted the nests that

165

lined the branches as far as his eyes could see. They were strip-mining near a nesting area. If the condition of the dozers meant anything, it appeared they had started a while back.

The birds would never return after man finished his mining, and the entire flock would perish if they couldn't find another area. He wondered if any of the babies made it before the dozers started scaring their parents away while raising the trees. It sure didn't look like it.

He turned towards the machines and looked to the sky with tears in his eyes. *How could anybody do this*, he thought as he sat on the cold, hard ground, putting his head in his hands.

The sun slowly started to set as Shree turned to John, pointed to the ground, and sat down. *She must be tired,* he thought. Judging from the sun, they had been running steadily for most of the day. *I could sure use a rest,* he thought. A squirrel raced in front of him and up a tree. "I thought they were all hibernating," he said, looking at Shree, remembering she couldn't understand him.

The squirrel chattered, and a second one answered from another tree behind him. *With the weather being warm, maybe they decided to stretch their legs*, he thought as the first squirrel took off, jumping from one branch to another. Seeing the first one coming, the second one ran in the opposite direction. It was too late. The chaser hit the chasee on the rear and immediately turned a hundred and eighty degrees, running and becoming the chasee. The chasee, now turned chaser, chattered again and ran after his friend.

Shree, noticing the game being played, jumped up and laughed a grizzly laugh. She chattered like the squirrels, and they stopped, looking at her and then at each other. She chattered again and lifted her arms towards the trees. They hesitated and slowly walked to her arms and down to her shoulders. John stood, mesmerized by what

166

was taking place. "*Aren't they wonderful?*" He heard her say as she petted them, and they jerked around her shoulder while watching him.

She lifted her arms back to the trees and chattered again. The chaser, deciding to play again, jumped over her chest, bit the chasee on the butt, turned, and ran back to the trees with the chaser following close behind. They ran off through the forest, chattering like Zach and Kirsten playing in the front yard.

I know I heard her say something, he thought. *Maybe this whole affair has finally gotten to me, and I'm going crazy.* She looked at him, pointed to her mouth to say food, and ran through the forest, leaving him alone. He looked around the ground and started to gather some wood.

He felt lightheaded, and his hands were shaking. He tapped his top pocket and pulled out his last cigarette. He pulled some wood scraps into a teepee shape and gathered some small sticks. *A nice hot cup of coffee would sure be nice.* He thought as he pulled the lighter from his pocket and lit his smoke.

Maybe she'll come back with something good to eat. I've had about all the roots and berries I can take. He resumed stacking the sticks on the wood chips and knelt on the ground. He flicked the lighter and lit the small sticks, watching the flames lick the wood.

Shree stopped her digging and stood alarmed. She sniffed the air, catching the scent of smoke. Visions of harsh flames ripping through the forest and the animals residing there entered her mind as she sniffed again. She sprinted in the direction the smoke was originating. She broke twigs from the trees as she passed them at breakneck speed and stood at the edge of the clearing where the yellow flame became visible. The yellow light created dark smoke rising into the air, and she could recognize John's body. He sat at the edge of the flames, warming his hands and staring into the dark trees, not seeing her. He put a stick with a red glow to his mouth, slowly breathing out smoke.

"No." She growled as she ran at the flames, kicking dirt into them. John jumped back, threw his cigarette to the ground, and watched, feeling like a little boy who had been caught with his hand in the cookie jar.

"Hey," he yelled.

Shree, satisfied that the fire was out, looked at him. He pulled out his lighter and held it in front of his face. "See," he started. It's Okay. Nothing to worry about." He flicked the lighter and smiled as the flames started to rise.

She looked at the lighter, horrified, and slapped it out of his hand. It flew, landing on the ground unlit. He started to protest, but knowing she couldn't understand him, gave up and sat on the ground pouting.

II-XIV

"Sheila," Phil yelled as he walked through the door, stepping into the living room. He stepped into the kitchen and walked towards the bedroom. "Sheila, I've got some good news," he sang as he opened the door, looking around. Apparently, she wasn't there. He walked back to the living room, turned on the television, plopped on the couch, and opened the beer he had grabbed on his way. He removed his shoes and looked at the phone as he stretched out, getting comfortable.

"No, Mrs. Montgomery. She wasn't here when I got home this afternoon, and I was starting to get worried. Yes, I know. Yeah... Are the kids doing all right? Good. Now...Well, listen. If they get to be a problem, you can bring them home. I'm not going anywhere, and... Okay, well, thanks again. Yeah, Okay...Bye." He hung up the phone and looked at the ticking clock. It was 8:00 p.m.

Where in the hell could she be? he wondered, getting angry. He walked to the refrigerator, opened the door, and looked for something to eat. He grabbed another beer from the top shelf and twisted off the cap, tossing it into the trash while guzzling the brew down his throat. He walked towards the television, flipped through the channels, and sat on the couch.

Hey," Sheila excitedly exclaimed as she walked through the door, closing it behind her.

"And where the hell have you been?" he angrily questioned.

"My, aren't we testy tonight?" she asked as she sat beside him. "Did you have a bad day or what?" She scooted closer and slid her fingers down his chest while kissing him on the lips.

He pulled back, smiling, and looked into her eyes. "I got a big contract," he exclaimed after promising himself he wouldn't say anything.

"What?"

"I got a big contract for work today."

"What are you talking about, Phil?" She blinked her eyes, staring at him.

"I was in the city today when I noticed some serious excavation happening on the outskirts of town. There were all of these big, expensive cars parked around it, and it looked like something important was happening."

He stood up, walked to the back of the chair, and pulled up his pants, becoming the man of the hour. "Well, I drove up to that site and asked who the owner was. I walked right into his office and I said to him, I said. 'I'm a general contractor with extensive experience building large structures, and anything you're building, I have a crew ready to go to work.' And do you know what they're going to build, Sheila?"

"No; what?"

"A hotel, Sheila, a great big beautiful hotel." He glowed with excitement. "He told me I had the job if I could get my crew there by Monday."

"But you don't know anything about building a hotel," she exclaimed, bursting his bubble.

"I know that, Sheila, but everybody has to start somewhere."

"But, what will you do when something happens, and you don't know how to handle it?"

"I don't know, Sheila; I'll worry about that when the time comes. Do you know how much the contract is for?"

She shook her head no as he pulled a paper from his pocket and unfolded it. "Go ahead, guess," Phil demanded.

"I don't know, Phil."

"No, really, guess."

"I don't know, twenty thousand dollars?" She shrugged her shoulders.

"Eight hundred and fifty thousand dollars, Sheila." He put the contract on the table as she stood with excitement overtaking her. "Eight hundred and fifty thousand dollars," he repeated as he pointed at the number on the crumpled piece of paper. "See? Right there." He turned it towards her, smiling, and took her hand. "Do you know what this means?"

She stood starry-eyed and threw her arms around him, jumping off the floor and wrapping her legs around his waist. "We're rich," she yelled, "rich!"

"Whoa," he cooled the conversation, "Not quite rich. But doin' pretty damn good." He laughed as he threw his arms around her and danced around the room.

"Cheers," she toasted as she put her freshly poured glass of wine in the air. "Cheers," he answered back, tapping the side of her glass with his bottle of beer.

She swallowed her mouth full of wine and stared at him, studying his face. She hadn't felt so secure and comfortable in a long time. She wanted to devour him and began fantasizing about the job he had found and the big house, shopping, and all the other things it would bring for her and her children.

"Yep, this could be the break of a lifetime," he gloated as he chugged the rest of his beer and belched. He looked at Sheila and thought about John as he stood and walked into the kitchen.

He sat down with his thoughts of John already forgotten. He threw his feet on the ottoman while handing Sheila the new glass of wine he had poured. He twisted the cap off his beer and threw it towards the trash in the kitchen, missing it. She poured wine down her throat as he chugged his beer and set it on the table next to him. Sheila sighed with a happy smile as she held her glass in her hand, laying her head on his shoulder, feeling like everything was going to work out.

II-XV

A large rock surged from the earth like a Dark Age castle. Shree climbed onto the rock that formed the cliffs they stood on, kneeled, and stared at the ground below. John kneeled beside her and followed her eyes into the distance.

He stood, thinking he spotted Roa-Ma, and quickly sat back down. A trail of their species slowly walked towards the fortress of rock, oblivious of his presence. Shree jumped up, grabbed John by the shirt, and returned him to the thick trees.

The mountains had come to life over the last few weeks. The snow finally melted, and the leaves returned to the trees. Everything turned so green. He had never seen so many different kinds of animals running through greenery and eating the feast that the end of spring would bring.

The rock structure grew larger as Shree slowly played her way through the trees, keeping a watchful eye on John. *Now, where?* He thought as they snaked through the trees. They had been walking or running all day. She was destroying him with all of this running, and he was ready to return to the cave to rest.

He looked down at himself and his dirty, ripped, and frayed clothes. He looked pretty good. With the limited berry and root diet he had been eating and the running this female put him through, he was feeling healthier and more robust than he had ever felt. His legs still ached, and he couldn't keep the same pace these animals could, but he was in the best shape of his life.

They approached a large crack that broke through the rocks. Shree carefully scanned the area and entered the narrow opening. John followed, entering and looking around as the sun peeked through the holes the giant boulders left, exposing a labyrinth of openings and pathways.

She carefully wound through the pathways, eventually reaching a room full of openings, all seeming to go through the thick rock wall. She stood momentarily and grabbed him, covering his eyes and entering the only opening that led to their final destination.

John closed his eyes as Shree put her hand over them. He opened them as she removed her hand, still unable to see. The cold, damp air worked its way through his bones, and a musty smell entered his nose. He spread out his arms, feeling the ice-covered rock surrounding him.

She grabbed his head and covered his eyes again as a light appeared in front of them. John sensed that their journey would soon come to an end. The sun blinded him as Shree removed her hand, and he felt the room become suddenly still. He tried focusing his eyes, wanting to see the presence he felt.

Twenty or so creatures resembling Roa-Ma stood, encircling him. A bear yawned in the corner, slowly pacing back and forth. Shree looked at him as she exited the cave, and the beings closed the opening behind her. He looked at the snow still covering the edges of the floor and then at the ice-covered walls in front of him. He looked at the sun in the sky above the dome where he stood. A group Roa-Ma's tribe broke apart, and he slowly walked towards the middle of the large, open room. They continued moving, exposing a large, intricately carved pot with a small fire burning beneath it.

Dear Lord, John thought as he looked at the glaring faces of the creatures tightening their circle, pushing him towards the pot.

They're going to eat me. A sweat broke above his brow, and his knees started to wobble as he came closer to the boiling substance, smelling the sour fragrance it produced. Roa-Ma appeared before him with an ancient bone crown on top of his head and a large, carved walking stick in hand.

He held the stick into the air, and a rush of power cleared John's mind, putting him in a haze and causing confusion within him. He looked at the beings as they made the circle ever tighter, and his confusion grew more intense. He lifted his arm, setting his hand in Roa-Ma's. The dream continued as the power surged, draining him of any remaining strength.

Roa-Ma looked at his stick being held high and quickly dropped it, slashing John's wrist. John pulled back, wanting to run and feeling his life's blood drain from him. Roa-Ma positioned John's fingers so he was making a fist. He held his fist in one hand and his forearm in the other, squeezing the blood through the cut and into the waiting mixture below.

Jon watched in shock as the blood dripped from his hand and into the potion below. Roa-Ma pulled out a series of large leaves and wrapped them around his wrist, stopping the bleeding and tying them down with the waiting vines. He smiled as he looked into John's eyes and led him to a rock altar. He sat him down and allowed him to fall to the floor. He lay there more out of consciousness than in and watched as the ritual continued.

The crowd broke towards the bear, and it slowly walked towards the pot and rock altar in the same confused state as John. It stood on its hind legs, releasing a moan as it lifted its arms, handing one of its paws to Roa-Ma. It looked at the creatures surrounding them as the stick came down, cutting the bear just above the joint of its giant claw, releasing its life-giving blood into the same soupy substance

John's plasma had joined earlier. The animal dropped to the ground, and the crowd reopened, allowing the animal to escape from the circle and into the cave that led outside.

John watched as Roa-Ma lifted the stick again, looking around at all of his brothers as if he were speaking to them. Sah appeared from the crowd, walking towards his father and kneeling before the large cooking brew. Roa-Ma walked to him and moved from side to side, looking at the leaders of every tribe. He looked at his son and dropped the stick before his eyes. Sah grabbed the stick, pulled himself to his feet, and looked at the other males.

He and Roa-Ma walked behind the large cooking pot, and Sah extended his hand to his father. The stick came down one final time, slashing both of their hands simultaneously. Their blood dripped, joining together in the ancient bowl. Roa-Ma scooped up handfuls of mushrooms, and Sah grabbed the roots and leaves sitting beside them.

They threw the ingredients in and reached down, picking up the cacti and other miscellaneous plants, including a large amount of the pain-killing plant Roa-Ma had used on his way home. Roa-Ma stirred as Sah added them to the boiling stew.

Sah grabbed the stick and took over, stirring the weird concoction as his father walked towards the others, addressing them again. He turned, looking at John, and raised him off his seat as he raised his arms.

John slowly walked towards him and stood beside the boiling pot, looking back at the audience. Roa-Ma dipped a large bowl into the brew and took a long drink. He exhaled his approval and passed it to Sah. Sah drank down the mixture, exhaling, and handed the bowl to John.

His stomach cramped, and he heaved some of the soup onto the ground. Laughter surrounded his head as the sweat poured from his face, and he faded in and out of consciousness.

A wolf howled as the thunderous sounds of a running bear approached him. It stuck its snout into his face and stood on its hind legs, towering above John. It growled, stretching out its massive paw towards him, ready to deliver a fatal blow.

It suddenly melted to the ground, glowing a bright red and turning to ash. A cold wind blew away the top layer of ash, exposing a snake and triggering a snowstorm that slowly began to cover his body. The snake sprang forward, and he winced, closing his eyes and throwing his arms in front of his face.

After not receiving the expected blow, he slowly opened his eyes and stared into a vast, crevassed desert. His father stood before him, fully dressed and holding a belt. His piano stood next to his father and shriveled to dust. It resurrected and stood again in defiance of his father, who disappeared.

The stars appeared above him, and Roa-Ma's face slowly appeared, with parts of it moving and the other parts catching up as if he were under a strobe light. Out of the corner of his eye, a flock of birds dove at him. He jumped around, facing them, and they disappeared into the night.

Roa-Ma looked at the man sprawling and jerking around on the floor. Roa-Ma stood holding his arms in the air and fell back to the ground. If he had known John would react like this, he wouldn't have given it to him. He wondered if he would pull out of the state he was in or if he would be the one to kill him before the night was through. He looked at the other males of his tribe. He looked back at Sah, who was busy contemplating and absorbing the wisdom of the elders as they discussed worldly problems in a room full of voices.

Roa-Ma sat staring at nothing as a scream faded from the mountains, and another answered it from farther away. He twisted his head, looking at the open dome above him, and howled into the night. John curled up, lying on the altar with skins covering him. He was shaking and still in shock from the events of the night, but the visions were slowing, and he was feeling more in control of his surroundings. Sah and the others left some time ago, and Roa-Ma had decided to stay with the man.

He turned his attention to the man and squatted between his legs, sitting, being still and silent.

A slow wind originated from their location, and chimes blew in the distance, filling the air with sounds and music. John suddenly felt calm, and he opened his eyes, looking at Roa-Ma's face.

A large, barren rock field opened in front of him, and a smaller version of Roa-Ma stood in the distance. The ground suddenly trembled, and a volcano smoked behind him. A creature resembling Roa-Ma lifted his nose in the air and sniffed as the ground shook and the mountain behind the missing link spat rock and flame into the air.

A small herd of antelope bounced in front of him and slowly navigated the rocks, making their way into the smoky distance. A porcupine scurried over his feet, trying to get to safety. The figure squatted and became anxious as three other figures appeared in the distance, tracking the animal that had just passed.

The figure lay flat on the ground, staying perfectly still as the other figures approached. John could see his short breaths and sweat rolling down his forehead. The others crossed the rocks and stopped just below the being and John. One of the approaching figures lifted his nose in the air and sniffed. His eyes locked onto John's, and he motioned for his friends to follow.

They had some of the same features as Roa-Ma's kind, but were obviously different. They were smaller and less stocky, with ornament-covered vines hanging from their necks and wrapped around their heads. They carried spears with chiseled rock tips and used skins for shoes. The calm demeanor and peaceful aura of Roa-Ma's Family were absent, and they ran excitedly and full of anxiety. They were the first Homo-Sapiens.

They reached the crest of the hill and looked down at the different races of man lying on the ground. They quickly circled him, and the leader kicked him in the head, grunting a command. The being jumped from the ground and stood, staring at John's ancestors. His chest heaved, and the fear of death showed on his face.

The leader grunted again and looked at his friends, who were smiling. They laughed back at him and took a step back as the leader quickly lifted the stick in his hand, hitting the unarmed enemy in the head. He fell to the ground as the primitive men closed in their circle, kicking and beating him with the sticks they held while stabbing him with the rock tips.

They grunted in triumph as Roa-Ma's features became apparent on the creature that lay bleeding and dying. John's ancestors laughed as they walked down the hill and resumed their perpetual hunt. Roa-Ma's ancestor exhaled one last breath as the blood poured from his body, forming a large pool of blood. His body twitched the remaining life out of it, and the ancient men disappeared over the horizon.

The scene began to fade, and Roa-Ma refocused as John slowly regained his senses, and the vision disappeared. He sat staring through Roa-Ma. "Oh God," he grunted as he tried to sit up with his stomach convulsing and its contents trying to make their way up his throat.

Roa-Ma's eyes lit up as the visions of men and the cities they lived in faded from his mind. The man twisted, facing the ground and leaving only bile as he vomited on the ground. Roa-Ma stood and walked before him, intently watching as his body convulsed.

"Are you feeling better?" Roa-Ma asked as John rolled on his back and closed his eyes.

"No, not much. In fact, I think I feel worse now than I have all day."

Roa-Ma stood in amazement, thinking the potion had gotten the best of him, too. "Tell me about your home."

Visions of Sheila, Zach, and Kirsten entered Roa-Ma's mind as John began talking about them with his eyes still closed and his trip continuing. Roa-Ma smiled, hearing every word the man was saying, and sat down next to him. He put his chin in his hands and braced them, his elbows sticking to his thighs. He intently stared at the man, studying his features, as they continued their conversation.

II-XVI

Phil began emptying the brown bags Sheila brought from the grocery store, placing food and condiments into the refrigerator and overhead cabinets. "These are garlic cloves," he growled. I needed garlic powder, or even garlic salt would have worked."

Sheila looked at him with her penetrating eyes and smiled. "I know, but it's all they had." She blinked and walked towards the couch, picking up a sleeping Kirsten and carrying her to her crib. She removed her coat, hung it in the closet, and walked to the kitchen, pulling out a bottle of champagne from one of the other bags.

Phil pulled the slices of toast from the oven and started stacking them on a plate as she approached him. "I thought we could celebrate you getting the business going and making enough money for us to live for a change." He looked at her, grabbed a handful of noodles from the colander, and tossed them onto a plate. He added the spaghetti sauce and tossed a piece of toast on the side.

The hotel job was going better than he could have hoped for. The bank loans were easy to obtain, and they allowed him to acquire whatever he needed to complete the job. He transferred some of the money from the job into investment properties and paid off all of Sheila's bills, allowing her to have some of the things she wanted.

The investments were something he always wanted to do. They were starting to become income-producing and were paying back the company, in materials, of course, that he had "borrowed" from the bank.

It had been almost a year since John disappeared, and the way it looked outside, it would only be a matter of time before the snow started falling again. The trees turned a spectacular array of yellows, reds, and golds, and the leaves began to fall. The hotel was more than half complete, and the man he was building it for had been introducing him to different builders since the job had begun.

Some were in high-ranking government jobs, and he had been made a few offers that paid very well. The problem was that the best offers were halfway across the country. As beautiful as Sheila was, something was starting to feel absent. The lovemaking wasn't what it used to be, and it seemed she was just another girl, like all the other girlfriends he had been with. He felt they were all there for the money and security he had to offer. The idea of him up and moving her and her kids wasn't an idea he wanted to undertake.

Thoughts of the single life were returning some fond memories, and the idea of staying was a commitment he knew he couldn't live with. His life was undergoing some amazing changes, and for the first time, he felt he was ready to make it on his own. He knew there was another life out there, with women waiting for him. She and her children had become a liability, and he knew he had to get away from where he was. He just didn't know how.

He looked at Sheila, who was busily munching on the spaghetti he had set in front of her, and then at the dishes stacked in the sink. He would miss her beauty the most. He enjoyed taking her out and being seen with her. *If it were another time, it might have worked.* She looked up at him and smiled as she sucked up the noodles, tipping her chair with a giggle. She was shy, yet had a way of being outspoken. Especially when she was drunk. Then, she was nothing but outspoken.

He looked at Zach and thought of Kirsten. He hadn't considered having children before, and they had kept his hands full since he started this relationship. She stopped doing anything around the house then, and now he found himself cooking and cleaning for them and bringing home the money. He thought *I'll tell her I'm giving the business back to her and moving on before this thing gets too serious. She's got some money now and should be able to make it without me.*

He fantasized about hiring another foreman and training him to run the company. If he could, his problems would be solved. *They were both so vulnerable initially that it was intense and went too fast.* Now, the longer it lasted, the more he felt uncomfortable.

Sometimes, it seemed as if John were watching everything they were doing. And there was no doubt in his mind that he wouldn't like some of those things. *She would have to understand.*

"What did you do at your grandma's house today?" Sheila asked Zach.

"Oh, nothing," he answered. "May I please be excused?"

She looked at him, squirming in his chair, and disgustedly exhaled. "Are you done?"

"Yes"

"I don't care; just make sure you wash your hands before you do anything else."

He jumped up, ran into the living room, turned on the television, and sat on the floor. "What did I tell you?" Sheila screeched from the kitchen sternly. Phil flinched, tired of listening to her yell at them all the time. She jumped from the table after being ignored and Ran to Zach, pulling him up and forcing him into the hall. He screamed in tears and walked the rest of the way to the bathroom crying. She sat back in her seat in a huff and picked up the toast, taking a small bite.

"Is there something bothering you?" she asked Phil quietly.

"No, I'm just tired." He paused. "I've had a rough day, and I still have to get payroll done so I can pay the guys tomorrow."

"I know you've been working hard, and I've been thinking. We've got a little bit of money now, so why don't we take a couple of days off and go somewhere? Just you and me. Mom said she'll watch the kids, and I'm sure everything will be Okay at your job while you're away."

He scooped the last bite from his plate and shoveled it into his mouth, standing and walking to the sink as she spoke. *He ran two crews, ten to twelve hours a day, and still did the books himself. He was looking for and bidding on other jobs to keep both crews working and was starting to feel overwhelmed.* Taking a few days off was the furthest thing from his mind. "I can't do that," he said. "There's too much to get done. And besides, I don't have anyone competent enough to leave in charge." He washed another plate and placed it in the dishwasher.

"Come on, Zach, it's time for bed!" Sheila yelled as she dumped her plate in the sink and walked towards him.

Phil was sitting at a calculator, busily figuring his payroll and wondering how he could break the news to her. *I've got to do it tonight*, he thought. He decided to wait until the kids were asleep in case there was a scene. Until then, he could keep himself busy with his paperwork. He signed another check and tore it out of the register, looking at Sheila sitting on the couch, watching television, and sipping her champagne. He knew there would be a scene. There was always a scene.

She jumped up, went back to the kids' room, tucked them in for the night, and walked into the kitchen, standing behind him. "How's it going?" she asked, opening the refrigerator and pulling out her bottle of alcohol.

"All right," he replied as she walked behind him and stood reading the paperwork over his shoulder.

"Looks pretty complicated to me," she said, sensing his irritation.

"This is just the beginning of it. Next, I've got to meet with people to secure the jobs, then I've got to be on the job site as much as possible to make sure I don't have any dead weight around and that the crews know what they're doing. Then there's workman's comp. My God, I could go on and on." He looked behind him and wondered why she never did what she promised, and taken over this part of the business. He wondered if she even understood what he was talking about. His resentment began to build, and he could feel himself becoming angry.

He sat down with her once to explain it and had been doing it himself ever since. She just couldn't get it. He turned back to his calculator, pushing more numbers. "But you get used to it," he mumbled, being too nervous to bring up what was really on his mind.

She looked at him and smiled. "Can you open this?' She asked, handing him the bottle of wine she grabbed.

"Damn it, Sheila, I'm trying to get some work done here, okay?" He took the bottle from her hand, plunged the corkscrew into it, twisted and pulled up, releasing the cork from it confines. The top came out with a loud pop. He held the bottle level as a fine white mist rose from the small opening the cork once occupied. He handed her the misting bottle and turned back to his papers. "Now, will you just leave me alone for a while?"

She stepped to the counter, pouring the wine into two glasses she had taken out earlier, trying to ignore his outburst. "Why don't you take a break for a while?" She smiled as she handed him a full glass of the nectar.

"I can't right now, Sheila. I've got to get this done."

"Oh, come on, one little glass isn't going to hurt you."

He stretched his arms, looking at her as she extended her glass for a toast. "Yeah, I guess you're right." *Now was as good a time as any to have their little talk.* He picked up his glass and took a sip.

"To you," she said, putting her glass in the air. He tapped his glass to hers, took a drink, and walked into the living room, sitting on the couch. She followed, sitting next to him.

He tapped his glass with his finger in time to the music on the radio as she nervously repositioned herself. They sat, not speaking. "I think we should talk," they said simultaneously, looking at each other and laughing.

"You first," Sheila said, still nervously giggling.

"No, you go ahead."

"No, really, Phil, I insist."

"No, it's really not that important. You go ahead."

"Well, okay," she said, stretching her arms between her legs and looking at the ground. "I don't quite know how to say this, but you know I haven't been feeling very well in the mornings for the past few weeks..."

She looked at the confused look on his face, hoping he would guess, and continued. "So, I went to the store this morning and bought this." Her hand trembled as she pulled a small white stick from her hand, setting it on the ottoman in front of them.

He picked it up, looking at it intently, still not knowing what it was. "So...?"

"So, it's a pregnancy test, Phil, and it's positive." She put her hands to her face, covering her eyes, and began to weep as a lump developed in his throat, and he swallowed. "I'm pregnant, Phil, and you're going to be a father." Her voice echoed through his ears, penetrating his brain, as he sat paralyzed, not knowing what to say or how to act.

III

Homecoming

III-I

John awoke to the sounds of growling. He slowly opened his eyes, expecting to see its origin, and rolled to his stomach, looking for the animal producing the sound. A mountain lion crouched over Shree, licking and biting the top of her head. Her hand came up, pushing the animal away. It became friskier, and she pushed it harder, throwing it to the ground. She growled something while rolling on her back, springing to her knees, and beginning to stand.

The trees had long lost their leaves, and the sky was dark. Small snowflakes intermittently fell around them. John shivered and wished they could start running again so he could warm himself. The deer and elk population increased with the coming of hunting season, as did the predators that followed their migration. The smaller animals were busy preparing for winter and trying not to be a meal.

The cougar swatted her on the rear, throwing her off balance. She tripped sideways and caught her balance as she pushed the animal off her and stood tall, glaring into its green eyes, chastising it. She never had to fight with this cat before, and there was something about it today that she didn't fully trust.

The big cat yawned, exposing its sharp white teeth, and trotted into the forest. Shree arched her back, stretching it, and looked at him. "*You're shivering*," she compassionately purred.

He looked at her with a quizzical expression on his face, once again feeling the effects of the potion he drank so long ago. The mountain lion returned, lying at her feet. It looked like the same animal that tried to kill him not so long ago. He looked at Shree and then back at the animal lying below her. The cat looked at him, yawning and exposing its great white fangs while licking its lips.

John walked towards a fallen tree and watched the cat as it dropped its head, resting it on its paws. The cat closed its eyes, ignoring his presence, and exhaled hard as if fully relaxed. Shree knelt next to the animal, rubbing its face and neck.

She momentarily looked at John and motioned for him to sit next to them. He shook his head no and stared at the ground, trying to clear his head and figure out how to get her to start running again so he could warm his body and get away from these predatory animals.

For being on top of the food chain, Shree thought, *they're sure afraid of everything.* She stood and walked to him, grabbing his hand and jerking him towards the cat. It opened its lazy eyes and watched them as they approached. Its mouth opened as it stretched its lips above its teeth, and a high-pitched sound emerged from deep within its throat as it yawned. It relaxed again, rolling on its side, and dropped its head to the ground.

John stopped in his tracks and stared at the sleeping animal. "*Isn't it beautiful?*" she asked.

He looked at her, startled and confused, feeling the dream again as a flashback from the drug drained through his mind. Dear God, please don't do this to me again, he pleaded in his mind as he watched her expression change, and she received no answer. She dropped her eyes and looked at the animal below.

She knelt down and rubbed the cat's neck, motioning for John to do the same. He knelt beside her and looked at the cat, still lying motionless. She grabbed his hand and laid it on the animal's thick coat. He stroked the heavy winter fur, and the cat heaved a sigh, stretching its legs and rolling onto its back, sticking its limp legs into the air and purring.

"The conversations you and Father must have had," he heard her say.

He leaned back and zoned into the countryside, second-guessing whether he had heard anything.

The cougar looked at him in anticipation momentarily and then dropped her head back to the ground. He looked at the now snoring cougar and continued stroking its fur. 'What?" he thought, feeling the strength drain from his body.

"He said he speaks to you and has learned much," Shree said, smiling while turning to look at him.

His thoughts turned to being taken from his family and forced to stay against his will. The pains of Sah tackling him and dragging him to the cave when he tried to escape were still fresh. He ran his hand through his hair and down the back of his neck. The cat looked up with half-opened eyes, sensing his sadness, and let his head slowly fall back, snoring again.

"Don't blame Sah," echoed through his head. "Until Father got well, he promised to keep you safe and alive."

"For what?"

"For doing what he did to you. Father has always believed that since we once communicated with your race, we could communicate with them again. He always believed we could find a way to reach your elders and stop the destruction of our world. I never believed it possible, but now I know anything is possible."

"But I don't remember?"

"You don't remember? Well...You were given our sacramental sustenance to open your mind on the day of Sah's ritual to make you

194

one with us." She looked over at the cat and around the trees. "All of us."

"I can remember little bits and pieces, but every time we talked, it felt like it does now. Like the night of Sah's ritual."

"That's interesting," she replied, trying to feel what he was speaking about, "but you aren't dreaming. You have been given a gift and need to learn how to harvest it. It will show you where to go and what is right for you. It will become easier as time goes by."

I knew we all came from the same place," she purred. "Our races, I mean. And it was said that we communicated in the beginning. But who would have thought?"

He looked at her, grabbing his full beard, feeling nothing, including the cold, and pulled to see if he could wake up. "I've seen the beginning."

She sat speechless for a moment and grew warm with knowing. "You saw the beginning?"

"Yes, the night of the ritual with your father."

She looked at him with a smile in her voice. "Father is the head of the elders and had just returned from a long journey when he met you. One of the boys from another tribe was having his ritual of life, and he was returning from that ritual, as well as the annual meeting of the elders."

"Our Mother was killed by someone like you before a season began about twelve years ago. I was young then and don't remember much of her." A tear welled up inside of her. "And even after that, he held onto the belief that our ancestors were right and that man could understand and accept our ways. "You've proven that."

"What?"

"You're capable of receiving communion, John. "

"Receiving what?"

"You see, John, when Father was showing you the beginning, it was from all of us. You had all of our thoughts, all of our emotions, and everything we possess. You possessed all that is now and will ever be within you. All that is seen and unseen. That's who we are. All of us."

"Communion is how we celebrate our cosmic connection to nature." Shree continued, "It's how we celebrate our creator and how we communicate with each other. It's how we communicate with the animals. You see, John, we all have the same creator, and with you having all of us, we had all of you."

"We could hear the thoughts of all mankind, from your leaders to your most minor children. In our writings, it states that your race and ours communicated. Lived together in peace and harmony. But the beginning was created when the first act was committed, and the confusion appeared. It acted as a force field, and we couldn't hear or see your race anymore."

"But you were the link, John, the one to bridge us back together. Your race abandoned communion when the beginning occurred, so they will never see us, and we can now understand why the force field existed."

"But now, we see your kind. We can track your kind. We can prepare for the final battle that is waging. Our species can now remain one step ahead and live to fight another day. We now know all your thoughts and movements. This is the greatest day in our history. And we owe all of this to you, John."

His weakness turned to fatigue, and he lay on his back, forcing himself to remain conscious. Everything looked different as his back relaxed, and his body faded in and out, creating the sensation that he was a detached mind floating above his body and seeing all. He

196

wondered if he was freezing to death as he closed his eyes, listening but not feeling the cold breeze blowing through the trees.

A loud middle C twang rang through his mind. Suddenly, the forest came alive with the sweet sound of orchestration as scales and arpeggios ran like a fox during a hunt. John opened his eyes and looked around. The snow began to fall, leaving cold, wet spots on his face. He slowly tuned out the world, falling into a deep sleep.

A gun blasted in the distance. John slowly opened his eyes and stared into the blackness, wondering where he was. He noticed a dull light coming from the undergrowth of an opening and walked towards it, realizing where he was. He pulled back the covering and stared up the tunnel leading to the main quarters.

Roa-Ma heard Sah imitate the bird's whistle and returned it with one of his own. The reverberation had occurred a little while ago, and he knew they were getting close to its origin. He stopped to catch his breath and gazed through the trees, searching for anything he could see.

Two men hunched over a large bull elk, busily chopping on the carcass and pulling out its insides. Their heads popped up every few seconds, looking around, ensuring nobody was watching.

Roa-Ma chattered like a squirrel, and Sah echoed a different voice back. He circled back to where the sound originated and stopped, freezing immediately and looking as if he had always been part of the forest. He spotted Sah squatting in the distance and sprinted to him. He knelt as he arrived silently. "Stay with them," he breathed. Put out a warning and make sure nothing else gets near them."

"Okay," Sah smiled, watching them carry their prize through the forest. Roa-Ma disappeared, and Sah took off, catching the men and mimicking their direction. This would be his first test since entering adulthood. He watched his father do these things a hundred times

197

before, and now they seemed natural and comfortable. He whistled in the voices of different birds and chattered like a squirrel as the men stopped, breathing in the cold air and looking around, feeling as though they were being watched.

Most of the animals learned to listen to the birds and squirrels when they sent their warning. A squirrel chattered at Sah a short distance away, and another after that, sending an echo of their voices through the trees. His father stood above the men, waving at him at the edge of a clearing and gesturing for him to stay where he was.

He disappeared into the trees, and in what seemed like an instant, Roa-ma stood in front of his son. "And I forgot to tell you," he announced before he arrived. "I need for you to get Ahm when you're done." He patted Sah on the arm to show his confidence and disappeared back into the rugged terrain.

The men before Sah struggled to hoist the animal's hindquarters back onto their backs and grabbed the antlers protruding from the deer's head. They lifted the elk off the ground and began trudging down the side of the mountain. He watched as they faded, and he followed close behind, sniffing the air and listening for other animals, including men, in the area.

They seem pretty deliberate with what they're doing, he thought. If they started shooting, he would continue the warning. Until then, he would follow silently while secretly watching and listening. Not attracting any attention to oneself had always been the safest.

Shree reached the cave opening and looked back at John, who was still a hundred yards behind her, breathing hard and stumbling in the fresh dusting of snow. She carried him home after he passed out yesterday, and when he woke up this morning, he seemed not to remember anything. It was as if their conversation had never taken place. With his sudden memory lapse, she doubted it had ever happened.

John stumbled, still breathing hard from their morning run, and fell to the ground. *Something is bothering her*, he thought, and if he couldn't figure out what it was, her constant running would surely kill him. They covered a lot of ground, and his legs were starting to feel like rubber. She looked at the cave entrance and then at John as she walked in.

Just like a woman, he thought *as she disappeared, kidnap me, bring me all the way here to the middle of nowhere, and then run me to death.* He laughed. He slowed his breathing and watched it rise above him as he raised his hand to his forehead, wiping away the sweat. He exhaled the air from his lungs and walked into the cave.

Shree walked to him and handed him a cup of water. "Thank you," he said, gasping for breath.

He drank the cold liquid and sat on the branch, grass, and leaf floor, still feeling light-headed as his endorphins slowly wore off. He leaned back and followed the wall to the ceiling with his eyes. Shree walked outside as John watched her. He lay his head back, closing his eyes, and she disappeared.

His thoughts drifted to Sheila, Kirsten, Zach, and the realities he had been taken from. It seemed like a lifetime had passed since that life. With this snow, he knew if he didn't figure out how to leave here now, it would be next year before he could. He looked down at his strong body and legs and knew he might stand a chance to get away from her during one of their runs. He turned, following her out into the dull gray sky. He sat by the entrance, too tired to follow, and watched as she disappeared into the forest, starting to plot his plan of escape.

Shree blended into the trees, continuing her deliberate trail and not noticing him. He sat on a tree stump sticking from the ground and stared into oblivion. He had been looking for familiar surroundings since they started. If he could remember which direction the strip-mining area was, he could start from there and follow the road to where it led. Now, if he could only remember. He stood and raced into the trees, hoping he was going in the right direction. He jumped over a stump and began to run, not seeing that Shree was not following.

When he found his way home, Shree was busily moving about the cave, organizing the twigs, leaves, and dead grass in an orderly fashion. He walked through the opening, cold, hungry, and frustrated at not finding his freedom. He wondered why she hadn't come looking for him and was thankful he found his way back to warmth. *Something must be happening tonight*, he thought. She looked like his wife when tidying up for someone's arrival and had a lot on her mind.

The sounds of the guns were silenced for now, and the snow continued to get deeper by the day. Time was running out for any kind of escape, and he figured he would be here till the spring. He looked at Shree, trying to get her attention and gauge the kind of reception he would receive, but he was still unable to understand why she hadn't followed him.

Roa-Ma walked through the entrance and watched his daughter. After a few moments, she noticed him and sat, trying not to show her anxiousness. "Is he here yet?" she asked, calming her voice.

"No, not yet," he answered. "And I wish he would hurry. If it gets any later, he'll have to spend the night and get started again in the morning. She smiled despairingly as she watched him turn around and walk back outside.

She continued to put food and supplies into a satchel, and John filled another one with water. He wondered who was coming and what new adventure awaited him with this new arrival. He studied the satchels, figuring they could produce at least a week's worth of food and water for him. It looked like someone was going on a journey, and he knew it was too cold for him to go alone.

Roa-Ma paced back and forth in front of the cave entrance, looking from side to side and searching the forest for every sound he thought he heard. A brownish figure caught his eye in the distance. He stopped and studied the area where the movement occurred, but could see nothing. The trees rustled, and in a second, Sah and another of their kind stood in front of him.

The third one stood a bit taller than Roa-Ma and appeared closer to Sah's age. His strength was shown by the rippling muscles of his chest and legs. His high cheekbones and low forehead set his features apart from Roa-Ma and his family, but they were of the same species.

"Ahm," Roa-Ma growled as he smiled and hugged the stranger. Ahm returned the affection, quickly pulling away from him.

"I'm sorry we're late, but I had to stay and help my father put out the cinders a small fire had produced. It didn't do much damage, but still took a while to put out." He lowered his head.

"That's okay," he stated. "I was just starting to worry and wonder whether you would make it tonight." He paused and looked at Ahm soberly.

"Are there any updates with the man?" Ahm inquired. "We haven't heard from you since Sah's rites of passage."

"Well, I think it's time to return him to his world. He has served his purpose, and I'll explain what happened after you return. We will have a meeting like no other." He got excited. "Everyone will come."

He tried to hold his excitement and not say too much. "So, I figured my future son-in-law would be the best man for the job." Roa-Ma laughed, patting him on the arm and staring into his eyes. "Besides, Shree has missed you and done so much in anticipation of your arrival.

"I know," Ahm replied. "And where is she anyway? Is she here?"

He started walking towards the entrance when Roa-Ma stretched out his arm and stopped him. "After we take this man back to his world, you're welcome to stay here and visit. But remember, I don't want any babies born until well after your wedding." Roa-ma laughed nervously. You're not married, and until you are, she's still my daughter." He leaned into his face, becoming serious and sticking his finger at him. "If you even think about touching her while you're here, I'll whip your butt and won't ever allow you back again. Understand?"

"Yes, sir, I promise," he said with his head down, showing respect. He put his arm around Roa-Ma, and they walked into the cave side by side.

202

III-II

Phil looked over the newly poured concrete foundation for the house they were starting to build. He followed his men as they poured the soupy mixture, patted and trawled the mud in overflowing troughs, and obtained a smooth finish. The three men working for him stood beside a wheelbarrow, dripping mud and holding their shovels. They coughed, smoked cigarettes, and gasped for breath.

The truck driver finished washing his truck and walked to Phil. He handed him a clipboard with a bill attached to it. "Here's the bill," he said as Phil grabbed it, shoved it in his pocket, and returned to his job. They said I was supposed to get a check or cash from you."

"What?"

"Yeah, they told me you knew."

"No, nobody said nothin' to me about having cash."

"Well, this is the first time you've used us, and it's our policy to collect during the pour. Don't you have a check or something?"

He looked at the man momentarily and motioned for his lead man to come and finish his job. "Yeah, hold on." He turned, walking towards his truck, feeling the man behind him. *God, where do they get these geeks from*? He thought as he opened his door and grabbed the checkbook from underneath the seat. He climbed in, opened the book, and sat down to write the check.

He took the clipboard from the driver's hand and scribbled his name on the bill with the pen that hung from a small chain. He clipped the check to it and handed it back to him.

"Thank you, sir," the driver smiled with a black-toothed grin. And thank you for using Quick-Mix." He started walking to his truck. "And call if you need us for anything else."

"Yeah, yeah," Phil mumbled as the driver climbed into the mixer truck and closed the door. "And kiss my ass." The diesel engine fired up and started running. The gears ground, and it slowly made its way through the few standing trees and onto the road.

"All right, guys," Phil yelled as he returned to the site. "Let's get some tarps over this thing, and then I'll line 'em up at the steer."

As Phil walked to his new truck, the men looked at each other, happy that it would be a night of drinking they wouldn't have to pay for. Phil climbed into his truck, popped the clutch, and headed toward the motel. He didn't know what he could do, but he needed a place to think.

This job had taken longer than he expected. With all the delays, he was beginning to question how much money he would actually make. Keeping this crew busy was all he could do, and he wasn't sure he could do that for much longer. The economy had taken a turn for the worse. His investments had gone south, and he had no way to pay back the money he used to "catch up."

The motel was three-quarters complete and had been lying idle since he ran out of money and drained what the bank would loan him. He was embroiled in lawsuits, and questions were being raised about embezzlement. He couldn't think of anything else but his problems. He had no idea how he would pull himself out of this or what he would do. All of his records had been subpoenaed, and he wondered what would happen when they found out he was working with a dead man's license.

He needed to get his own general contractor's license and fast. He hadn't been charged with anything and didn't want his parents to know what he'd done. He had been sending whatever they requested and thought he would figure out what he could do while appeasing them. His appeasements had become futile. When he returned home last night. He received a letter requesting his appearance in court within thirty days. He prayed for a miracle and a reasonable attorney. If only he could stay ahead of the banks and the courts.

When word hit that he would be unable to finish constructing the hotel, all the jobs he had been offered were pulled. With Sheila being pregnant, he decided to do the "right thing" and turn down any job he was offered out of town. Unfortunately, no one ever called to test his dedication.

Winter was here, and he felt his surroundings closing in on him. He had to figure out what to do about these legal matters, and he had to do it now. He didn't want to go to jail, and his fear would grow stronger as the days went by. His whole world was falling apart, and his emotional state followed closely behind.

Too big, too fast, he thought. And it would cost him everything he worked so hard to get. It could put him in prison and take away his freedom. The Houlton bid was the only job he knew he had coming up in the near future, and if that one fell through, he was screwed. He had to start beating the bushes and bidding more jobs. It was just so hard for him to get motivated.

The sun blazed into Phil's eyes, forcing him to pull down his visor. He pulled onto a dirt road and punched it, heading forward. The bulldozers ahead were stirring up dust and throwing it in the air, cutting down the visibility. He turned left, and the unfinished motel towered before him. He pulled up to the front door and got out, walking up the stairs to the office.

He pulled the keys from his pocket and tried to insert them into the handle. They didn't fit. He tried every key on his ring, trying the one he knew was the right one five or six times before giving up. "Damn it," he sighed as he stood up, putting the keys back in his pocket. He ran his finger down the wall and carefully checked it for flaws, thinking about what could have been and how he could have been so stupid to screw this up.

Sheila was busy cooking as the sun crept below the mountains. Phil would be home soon, and she wanted his dinner ready when he arrived. She set the oven to 375 degrees and opened the cabinet door above her. She pulled down her bottle, poured some into her glass, and set it back in the cabinet. She grabbed the candles and holders behind it, replaced the bottle, and silently closed the door. She sat down and crossed her legs, bouncing her free foot up and down as she placed the candles on the table.

She woke to the sound of Kirsten crying and looked at the clock on the wall. It was 11:30, and Phil still hadn't bothered to come home. She sat up on the couch, regrouping her senses, and walked to the table, blowing out the burning candles. She pulled her bottle from the cupboard, took a drink, and fixed a bottle of juice to quiet the baby. She chugged down the straight alcohol and walked back to the children's room, giving her baby the juice and lying down next to her.

The alarm's constant tone ran through her dreams, finally waking her. She rolled over and climbed over Kirsten, touching the floor, and then ran to her room to turn off the incessant noise. She stood looking at the clock with her heart pounding from the run. It was five am.

She looked at the empty bed, seeing Phil hadn't returned. She walked to the kitchen, filled a cup of water from the sink, and chugged it down. She walked to her bed, pulled down the covers, and crawled in, flipping on her stomach. She lay there staring at the clock, angry at Phil and thinking he was with another woman.

Sheila rattled the pans around in the cabinet until she found the right one, clanged it out of its hiding place, and placed it on the stove. Zach and Kirsten quietly sat in the living room watching the television, ignoring the noise that blasted behind them. She felt like she hadn't slept last night and couldn't get back to sleep after she got up to turn off the alarm.

Sheila rolled around obsessing about her thoughts and finally gave up the fight, forcing herself out of bed around six. She made coffee, cleaned up the uneaten dinner, and had been drinking ever since. She walked to the refrigerator and opened it, pulling out the sausage and eggs from within.

She stared at the door momentarily, wondering if Phil was still alive and imagining him again with another woman. She walked to her cabinet, pulled down the bottle of Vodka, and poured more into her coffee. She gulped it with a shaking hand.

The water splashed into the sink as she rinsed the breakfast dishes and placed them in the dishwasher. She remembered the day John brought it home. It took him over two weeks to fix and install it underneath the counter.

She lost all but one drawer and most of her under-the-sink storage. She hated it, and watching him gloat made it even worse. It took him over two weeks to get over himself when his accomplishment was complete. But now she missed him and thought of how funny he was then.

Phil opened the door and walked in. Kirsten jumped up, running to him and grabbed his leg, not wanting to let go. "And where the hell have you been?" Sheila yelled from the kitchen.

"I'm sorry, hon, but Steve and I took a guy out last night who wants us to start a house for him in a couple of weeks. He got me so drunk that I could hardly walk. When I finally woke up, I was at Steve's, and it was morning. I'm really sorry."

"You mean Steve doesn't have a phone?" she slurred, stumbling out of the kitchen and getting in his face.

Oh my God, she's drunk, he thought, feeling like he needed some sleep to regain his strength before this fight got started. "I'm sorry, Sheila, but you don't understand," he whined as he looked at her. Her four months of pregnancy were starting to show, and her belly was beginning to protrude. "But when I say that I couldn't walk, I mean I couldn't walk."

"Don't give me that crap," she screamed, pushing him and stumbling backward for a moment, regaining her balance. "I know you, Phil, and you would go running off with any young thing that you thought would have you," she giggled, thinking she made a joke, and gulped down more of her Vodka. "You're such a piece of shit!"

"Sheila, please. I'm really not feeling very well..." The phone rang in the living room. He looked at her, angry and tongue-tied, and then at the phone as it rang again. "Are you going to answer that?" he yelled, being thankful he had been saved by the bell.

"Hell no," she emphasized as she plopped down on the couch, trying to be rebellious. "I'm not your maid.

He walked to the phone and picked up the receiver. "Hello..."

"This is the Tree Line County Sheriff's Department," he heard the nasal voice recite from the receiver. "Is there a Mrs. Pierce there?"

"Yeah, hold on a second," he said as his heart began beating wildly. He pulled the phone from his ear and handed it to Sheila. "It's for you."

"Hello," she slurred out. "Uh-uh," she nodded, trying to sober up at the sound of the officer's voice. "Are you sure it's John?" she screeched. "Well, okay, but where did you find him?" She nodded her head again, and a tear formed in her eye. "Okay. Well, thank you for calling and letting me know. I'll head that way as soon as I can." She set down the phone and buried her face in her hands. "Oh my God," she screamed before breaking into hysterical crying. "They think they've found John."

Phil scooted next to her, trying to comfort her and determine whether any of his thoughts were true.

"They want me to come to the station as soon as I can to identify the body." She buried her head into his shoulder and continued crying as a wave of relief passed through his body. He put his arms around her, pulling her towards him, allowing her tears to flow.

III-III

John ran across the ground, slipping on the icy snow and slamming onto his butt. He sat there, feeling like he had broken his tailbone and holding his breath from the pain. They had been trudging through the snow and running for three days now, stopping only when the forest became black. The forest was darkening now, and this was where they would sleep for the night. He wondered where they were going and had been watching Ahm more intently as the days passed.

A light flashed from the corner of his eye, and he moved his head in that direction. He moved his hand to his lower back and exhaled as he pushed on it. *What the hell was that?* he wondered, sitting there, feeling the pain from his lower back as it flashed again. *A roadway*, he thought, wanting to run while looking at Ahm sitting next to him. He wouldn't make it very far.

He wondered if his companion had seen it and excitedly searched in the direction from which the light had appeared, as it flashed again. He quickly focused his attention on Ahm, not wanting to alert him to what he saw. Ahm stared in a different direction, apparently oblivious.

A squirrel hopped onto a branch above his head and began to chatter. He jumped, startled by the noise, and looked into the tree. The squirrel looked at him with a tilted head and ran back to the trunk. It appeared again, peering down at him and jerking on the branch, ready to run.

Something excited this little guy, he thought, trying to divert his thoughts and eyes from the road as Ahm sat next to him, staring into the dark. *He would run the first chance he had,* he thought, as excitement overtook him at the thought of being home. He looked at the tiny animal, trying to chatter back.

The squirrel raised its head and jerked in different directions, running down the tree and touching John's leg. It quickly turned around and ran back up the tree, stopping at the same branch and twitching nervously. John looked up, smiling, and stared the animal in the eye.

The forest fell quiet, and faint chimes began to ring through the trees. An upbeat rhythm and blues bass line began, and the forest burst alive with sound and music. The squirrel ran down the tree and ended up in his lap, becoming still and content. He started to stroke the small animal's coat and zoned, staring blankly into the trees and listening.

Ahm watched him, amazed. "Shree has taught you well," he said, looking into his eyes and touching him and the squirrel.

"Yeah, I'll make sure to tell her that when we get back," John said.

"What do you mean when we get back?" Ahm asked as John sat there silently. "Didn't anybody tell you where we're going?"

"No," jumped into his mind as the man slowly turned his head his way. "Where are we going?"

Ahm leaned his head back and thought for a moment. He took John's head in his hands and stared into his eyes. "I've come to take you home, brother." He smiled. "Those lights that you've been seeing are where your people live. I'll take you as close as I can, and then you're on your own."

Strength began draining from his body as feelings of overwhelming relief overtook his senses. *You're going to take me home*, he thought, feeling his throat swell and trying to stop tears from appearing in his eyes. "My God, I'm going home." He sat silently, thoughts of his family flashing through his mind, and a feeling of uneasiness about returning.

"Yes," Ahm said. "And I'm sure your family will be happy to see you."

"And what of Shree and Roa-Ma and Sah? Why didn't they say goodbye to me?"

"They did. When we were leaving the cave, they all said goodbye."

John thought back to Roa-Ma and Sah grabbing him by the shoulders and looking at him before they left. He thought of Shree handing him the supplies they prepared earlier, taking her time and moving as if she were sad. He had no idea what was happening and wished he could have heard what they said.

"And we'll all be okay, Ahm started, "I'm going to marry Shree." He straightened his posture, proud of this statement, and continued. "That is if another territory ever opens up." He picked up a rock and tossed it, striking a tree with a snap as it bounced off. "When Sah was sent to bring me here, I hoped Roa-Ma had some news about an open territory." He stopped, shrugged his shoulders, and sighed. "I just hope one opens soon."

"Another territory?"

"Yes, we all live and protect separate areas, and each area only allows one family. So, we must wait until a territory opens up before we can get married and move to it. I suppose that's our way of keeping our population under control. My brother has been promised my father's territory when he dies, so if another doesn't open, I'll die and never be able to be with Shree." He stared at John with eyes that seemed defeated. 'I was hoping this was why I was called and why you were here."

"How could I be involved in another territory opening up?"

"Who knows?" I thought maybe you were an elder that Roa-Ma captured. I hoped you two reached an agreement about opening something and letting us restore it. It's all I could think about on the way here, but I can see it isn't how I thought."

He paused and looked at John. "He had talked about these things in the meetings of the elders," Ahm continued. "He believes there's a way to bring your race and ours together. That we could someday learn to live in peace and harmony." He laughed. "Father thinks he's crazy and should step down from the council. But the younger of us believe in him and hope he has the key to the day we no longer have to hide." He paused, watching John as he drifted in and out of consciousness.

"Stories of old," he continued, "tell of a time when the forest will be no more. We will be hunted for our hides, and the animals will be lost forever. Slowly, I see the prophecies coming true. We must have some help in keeping our forest alive, or eventually, none of us will be able to live." He looked at John, feeling his exhaustion and sensing that he wouldn't understand much longer.

"Well, maybe there's something I can do." John's voice faded in and out.

Ahm's face lit up with hope as he pieced together his voice.

"I'm not sure what I can do." John's thoughts came in and out like a radio losing its signal. "But I'll try. I promise that I'll try."

Ahm looked at the ground and slowly stood, stretching his back. "I need to look around and scout where we're going. We'll have to leave pretty soon if we're going to make it before nightfall." He tapped the squirrel from John's lap. It scrambled up the tree and into the darkness from whence it came.

John stretched out onto the cold, hard ground and stared into the darkening sky. Music resonated through the forest like the symphonies in the music halls he once dreamt of playing. "I'll try." Ahm could hear him slur again as he continued to run out of sight.

John slowly woke to the sun on his face and the sounds of people screaming and yelling nearby. He looked around, regained his senses, and looked at Ahm sitting beside him. Ahm looked at him, touching him on the shoulder as he sat up. Ahm stood, pointing his hand, and crouched down, looking John in the face, hoping he would understand. He stood up, pointed in the same direction again, and walked towards the trees in the opposite direction. He looked at John one last time, smiling and waving his hand in the air. "Please help us," he screamed at John's deaf ears before disappearing into the trees.

John turned and trudged down the mountain, following the sounds he could hear. He reached a break in the trees and looked out over the unnatural opening, glistening a sparkling white. A skier whooshed in front of him, and the hill came alive with the people and sounds he heard while sitting with Ahm.

He ran his fingers through his long, grizzly beard and started walking down the hill, watching the people stare at him as they slid by. He wondered what he must look like and felt his tears coming back as he saw a large brown cedar-sided building in the distance with ski lifts in front and on the sides of it. *I'm home*, he thought, *I'm finally home.*

High above the long clearing John had reached, Ahm stopped and watched him descend the slope. *I sure hope Roa-Ma knows what he's doing*, he thought. *This could begin the hunt that wipes us out and destroys the only world we've ever known.* He turned and bolted through the forest with thoughts of his time with Shree filling his mind.

John reached the clubhouse and walked inside. He felt in a haze as he looked around at the people inside. The ones he got close to turned and walked away, disgusted with his reeking smell and appearance. He froze as people quickly exited in different directions, rushing for the doors. An employee cautiously walked towards him. "Can I help you with something, sir?" he asked, trying to hold his breath after smelling the stench a few steps back.

"Why yes," answered John, trying to be professional and keep his composure. "I need to use a phone and find a place to get cleaned up." He felt inside his pockets, trying not to be obvious about it. "But I don't seem to have any money now." He looked at the man and smiled, tears welling up in his eyes.

"Listen," he began in confidence after getting no response.

The man slowly breathed out and was forced to breathe in. He could think of nothing except the smell as he watched John's mouth move, not hearing his words.

"I know how I must look, John continued. I'm sure this is a very weird situation for you, but it's been a long time since I've seen any kind of human civilization."

His tears began to flow as he became desperate with the man, wishing he were back in the forest with Roa-Ma and his family. "Please help me out here, and I'll pay you back as soon as my wife hears I'm okay and comes to pick me up, okay?"

The man stood expressionless as John stopped talking, jumping at his chance to escape. "Please wait here, sir." He turned, exhaling the breath he was holding, and quickly walked up the stairs. He walked to a door marked manager and knocked, waiting for a response.

"Come in." A voice rumbled from within.

The employee poked his head in and smiled. "I'm sorry to disturb you, sir," he began, "But I think we have a situation developing in the lobby demanding your immediate attention."

"Situation?"

"Yes, sir. There seems to be a mountain man who has wandered into our place of business, and he needs to be dealt with now."

"A mountain man? What do you mean, a mountain man?" He looked at the missing person poster that had been pinned to his wall for the past year. "Do you think it could be him?" He pointed to the picture.

"Hard to tell, sir. You'll just have to come and see for yourself."

"And why can't you deal with this situation?" The manager asked, standing from his chair and exhaling a sigh.

"I just think you would handle this better, sir."

"Well, I guess I'll have to go down there and talk to him at once to hear his story." He brushed off the lapels on his suit and started for the door.

"But sir, I should warn you..."

The hotel manager turned, standing in the doorway, and looking at the man, "Don't bother me, Whitley; I've got much more important things to do than listen to your constant talk and handle things like this for you." This man is probably nothing more than a vagrant looking for a handout. He walked out and headed down the hall. "Have security alerted in case he should get out of control." His voice faded as he continued walking and making his way down the stairs.

He spotted John from across the room and approached him briskly. "Hello, sir. My name is Mister Bradley, and I'm the manager of this establishment. Is there something that I can do to help you?" His nostrils curled as he breathed in from his long sentence. He looked at John in horror and disbelief. "My God, man," he blurted

216

out as he held his breath and quickly walked away, looking for his missing security.

"Yes, there is," John began, desperately chasing after him. He watched the man climb back up the stairs. "I've been away for a long time," he yelled, walking to the bottom of the stairs and looking at the manager with a lump forming in his throat. "And if you would just allow me to call my wife, I think we can clear this up!" He screamed louder as the man reached the top of the stairs and turned around.

A quarter flipped down the stairs as security arrived, surrounding him. "The phone's down the street," Mister Bradley yelled from the top of the stairs. "And there's a bathroom in town as well. It's at most five miles down the road.

He turned his attention from John and looked at the head of security. "Get him the hell out of here before he scares any more of our customers away. Then call the police and tell them another one of those homeless people is on their way into town and needs to be dealt with as soon as possible."

"But I'm not a homeless person," John protested.

The large man nodded his head in agreement with the manager and motioned for the rest of the guards to follow him as he escorted the culprit outside into the cold. The manager walked back to his office, cursing Whitley for not warning him about the smell the man excreted. He slammed the door and sat at his desk, picking up the phone and making sure his orders had been followed.

"But I haven't done anything," John screamed as they pushed him out the door. "I really just need some help."

"The town is down that road that way," the man who pushed him outside exclaimed as he pointed in the direction of a town. He turned to walk back inside. "That way," he repeated, pointing again. He slammed the door and disappeared.

John stood stunned, looking at the quarter in his hand and the closed door in front of him. He turned, looking down the road the man had pointed to. He took a step, starting to jog, and heard sirens in the distance.

III-IV

Sheila hurried around the house, putting things away and picking up various knick-knacks and paintings that she and Phil had bought together. She picked up a bear holding a heart that said, I LOVE YOU THIS MUCH. And remembered the day they took the kids to the Carnival, and Phil won this for her.

She really didn't want to go and would have rather stayed home, but Phil and the kids talked her into it, and she was glad she went. The kids had so much fun on the rides and playing the games on the midway, and it warmed her heart to see them laugh. Phil won this for her after winning other stuffed animals for the kids. It must have cost him hundreds of dollars to win the small toys the kids forgot about the day after they got home, but he ensured they had them.

She placed it in the large trash bag holding the other things she had picked up along the way and broke into tears like she had been doing all day. She walked to the kitchen counter, regaining her composure, and closed her bag of mementos. She sealed it by wrapping a twist-tie tightly around the opening, stood, placed the bag on the kitchen table, and walked into the living room. Her mind became consumed with thoughts of John returning home.

Zach played outside, oblivious to what was happening, while Kirsten lay on the couch watching television, not feeling well and nursing a cold. She thought about explaining the situation to them, but knowing Zach's hyperactive tendencies, she decided it could wait

219

until they reached the police station. By then, Zach could burn off some energy, and Kirsten could rest and store hers.

She walked into the living room, checking on her little girl. She lay on the couch, watching cartoons and sucking her thumb, slowly drifting to sleep. Sheila walked to Kirsten's bedroom, grabbed a blanket, and wrapped it around her, kissing her forehead and thinking of how excited she would be to see her father.

After the police department called the night before, their words took a while to sink in. She went into shock and could see her life crumbling before her. She was happy that John was still alive, but she didn't know what to say or how to explain what had been happening in his absence.

She had been drinking all day and was on the verge of blacking out when they called. She just wanted to get off the phone and didn't know why she told Phil what she did. The words she heard were not what she told him, and John was alive.

She thought about what the police station had said and, feeling like she was coming to terms with the situation, told Phil the truth. He called them, not believing her, and the fight started again.

It had been a rough night, and she passed out after the yelling calmed down, listening to him talk about the situation they were in and what they were going to do about it.

They found John at a ski area a hundred miles from where he disappeared. They planned to dispatch a car for him in the morning and needed her to pick him up at the station in the afternoon. He was busy at the other police station getting cleaned up and being checked for trauma, or he would have called personally. But he did want them to tell her he loved her and couldn't wait to see her again.

She had to remove all of Phil's things before he returned. She drank more of her cold coffee and Vodka and looked at the clock through teary eyes. *Oh God*, she thought as tears rolled down her face. *What am I going to do? I thought he was dead*. She looked at her bulging stomach and walked into her bedroom, looking at herself in a full-length mirror and turning sideways. She broke into tears at the sight of her belly and sat on the bed sobbing.

She regained her composure and stood as she heard the front door slam. Wiping tears from her eyes, she stared down the hall, expecting Phil.

"What's the matter, Mommy?" Zach asked as he appeared in the hall and walked through the door of her room. He sat on her bed, and she put her arms around him, giving him a hug. She suppressed her crying and gently moved her hand up and down, lightly scratching his back.

"Nothing, honey," she whispered. I'm just crying because...because I'm happy, that's all." She stared into his eyes and tried to smile as her tired, bloodshot eyes betrayed her. Now, let's get your shoes on and put your sister's on too. We have to go for a ride now, okay?" She stood, pulling him from the bed and pushing him toward his room.

He shot down the hall and disappeared around the corner. "Don't forget your sister," she yelled as his footsteps stopped in the kitchen. "And stay out of the cookies!"

He sighed, exasperated, wondering how she always knew what he was doing, and walked into the living room. He picked up his sister, walked to the bedroom, and set her on the ground. She squealed as Zach climbed into the closet, digging through their toys and a pile of clothes in search of her shoes.

I've got to get out of here, she thought, listening to Kirsten laugh at her brother. *And where the hell was Phil?* She had to find him. She entered her bedroom, scanning for any objects she had left behind, and walked back down the hall, looking at the kids as she went by.

"We're ready," Zach yelled.

She grabbed their coats, handed one to Zach, and put on Kirsten's while trying to calm her crying. She picked Kirsten up, turned around, opened the door, and walked into the cold, foggy morning.

She spotted Phil's truck sitting on the side of a storage building and screeched around the corner into the lumber yard. *Well, it's about time*, she thought as she slammed the gears into neutral and stepped on the parking brake. She had driven all over town and gone to his work sites. She was ready to give up when she came here out of one last hope.

"Okay, Zach, now do Mommy a favor and watch Kirsten. I'll be back in a few minutes." She jumped from the car, ran through the parking lot, and entered the store.

"And I'm telling you that I've got to have my materials tomorrow," she heard Phil say as she walked through the door.

"And until my computer tells me you've made a payment, you can't have anything," the manager said as she stood from her chair and walked to the counter. I'm really sorry, Phil, but this one's out of my hands, and yelling at me isn't going to do you any good."

Phil turned around and stomped out, flabbergasted. He stopped, stunned to see Sheila, and walked to her. He looked at her, surprised, and grabbed her by the shoulders. "Hey, babe, what's up?" he asked, stepping out of the store with her.

"What was that all about?" she asked.

"Oh, something about her dumb ass computer. If it wasn't the only place in town, I wouldn't even do business here." He looked at Sheila's swollen eyes. "What are you doing here anyway?" he asked as they exited the door, leading her to her car.

"I can't do this by myself," she sobbed.

"Well, you're going to have to, Sheila. We talked about this last night, and I have too much work to do here. There is no way I'm going to confront him about all of this right now."

"You have to, Phil. I just don't know if I can look at him and tell him what's happened." She lowered her head. "It is your baby, Phil, and I need you to be there with me."

"You know, Sheila, this is all your fault anyway. He yelled, feeling trapped. "You're the one who seduced me, and you're the one who got pregnant."

She leaned on her car and started to cry again, looking at him and clinching her fists. "This is not all my fault, Phil; you know damn good and well that you are as responsible for this as I am."

"You have never lived as good as you have with me," he boasted. "He could have never done the things that I have for you."

She regained her composure and grabbed the car door. "You're such a piece of shit, Phil, and I don't know what to do." She opened the car door and stepped in.

He grabbed her before she could enter and spun her around, looking into her eyes. "Are you going to divorce him then?"

"I don't know what I'm going to do."

He threw his hands in the air and slammed them down on the car's roof, understanding their situation. "This is really crap!" he yelled, looking at her. "How could this be happening?'

"You have to go with me."

"I can't, Sheila," he whispered, remembering the court problems he was about to confront. He just wanted to put them off forever, but he could feel the noose tightening around his neck.

"But we have to figure out what we're going to tell him," Sheila said, hating how he was handling this and wishing he would stop being such a baby.

"What time do you get him?'

"Four O'clock."

"So, what do you think we should tell him?" Phil asked for the hundredth time as they drove to pick up John. The pain in his stomach got worse as they got closer to the police station, letting him know it was time to figure this problem out.

"I don't know." She started, tears forming in her eyes again. She sat in silence for a moment, thinking. "I guess the truth is pretty obvious," she finally said, holding out her belly.

He watched her begin crying again and became irritated. This had been going on all day, and she still hadn't answered his question. "Listen, Sheila," he said, trying not to show his anger. "It's three thirty, and he will arrive at the cop shop at four." He gritted his teeth and raised his voice. "Now, I think we need to talk about this. Will you tell him it's over with you and him?"

She pulled herself up in the seat and fixed her posture as she copped an attitude and made a decision. "Then we'll tell him the truth and let him decide." She turned her head, not wanting the subject brought up again, and stared out the window, twirling her hair with her finger.

"But Sheila, what are we going to do about us?"

"We'll just have to tell him the truth, that's all," she screamed again as he leaned his head back and tuned her out. "And when we get there, you could be the man and start the conversation." He watched the countryside and his life race by him, stopping at a place he had never dreamed of.

John's heart raced as he looked out the window, and his town's City Limits sign rushed by. He put his hands behind his head, anticipating seeing his wife and children. He thought of his wife often while he was with his temporary family, and the idea of being alone with her in his bed sent butterflies growing in his stomach. He fantasized about the reception he would get and the look on his children's faces as he got closer to home.

The black and white car turned left onto a side street, and the police station loomed ahead. They pulled to the curb and stopped at the front door. A uniformed police officer exited the car and opened the back door, where John sat silently..

"Here we are, sir. Your family should be somewhere on the second floor."

He stepped from the car, running his hand over his clean-shaven face, and looked at the new suit of clothes the government bought for him, now covering his body. He took the policeman's extended hand and gave it a firm shake. "Thank you." He smiled with an ear-to-ear grin. "Thank you so much."

He turned to the other officer, grabbed his hand, and shook it too. He let go and slowly walked up the stairs with his new friends behind. He rubbed his hand back over his face, feeling and smelling cleaner than he could ever remember. He reached the door and walked through.

"I thought I'd never see this place again," he said to the men standing beside him and holding the door. "You know, things have got to be pretty rough when your hometown police station looks good." They laughed as he put his hands in his pockets, and they picked up their pace. They walked up the stairs, and the officer in front of him opened the door to his final destination.

"Daddy, Daddy," Zach yelled as they walked in. Kirsten waddled behind him, shaking her hands in front of her, smiling with hyperactive excitement. She looked at the man in front of them, confused at her brother's reaction, while feeling the emotions of her mother and Phil.

John knelt down, picking up and hugging the running Zach in one arm as Kirsten slowly approached, satisfied with her brother's welcome. He reached for her with his other hand and lifted her to their level. He held them tightly and kissed them while looking at his wife and friend. Tears of joy ran down his face, and he gleamed from his children's excitement, looking at Sheila.

His joy turned sour, and his face frowned as he looked at them, knowing something was wrong. He looked at Phil and sat down with the kids, who were looking at their mother.

"John," Phil exclaimed as he extended his hand and grabbed him with the other, detouring his path and hugging him. "We really missed you."

John hugged him back, patted him on the back, and continued to look at his wife. *She's put on some weight*, he thought. He broke away from Phil with all politeness and headed her way. "What's the matter?" he asked, putting his arms around her and holding her tight. "Aren't you glad to see me?"

Her body trembled as she embraced him, returning his affections. "Of course I am." She smiled. "I've missed you so much."

She cried as he pulled away from her and looked deep into her eyes. Her lip started to tremble, and tears ran down her cheeks. Her peripheral vision could see Phil in the background, looking at her as John leaned in, trying to kiss her. She started crying, pulled her face from his, and ran through the door. Her wailing continued as she ran down the hall, not knowing where she was going. Phil was supposed to protect me, she thought as she ran down the stairs and reached the door that took her outside.

"What the hell is going on?" John asked as he looked at Phil and then at the officers. Phil shrugged his shoulders and opened his mouth, but nothing came out. John turned, ran through the door, and followed his wife.

He followed his earlier path through the police station, hoping she had run outside. He ran out the front door into the dimming light, squinting his eyes and looking down the stairs. Sheila leaned against the railing that rose from the concrete at the bottom. Her body heaved as she breathed, and tears rolled down her face.

He walked to her, putting his arm around her waist and pulling the hair from her face. "What's the matter, Sheila? I don't understand. I haven't seen you in over a year, and you treat me like you don't want me here."

A sharp pain entered her stomach as she looked at him, still gasping for breath and wincing from the pain. "It's just that it's been so hard without you." She leaned over the railing, throwing up the contents of her stomach as he held her hair and watched.

She stood and looked at him, wiping her mouth, feeling like she might do it again. She threw her arms around him, and he could smell alcohol on her breath as she continued crying and holding him tight. "I'm just not feeling very good right now, and all I really want to do is go home."

They pulled up to the small tin home, and John stared at it, remembering it being bigger. He looked at Sheila sleeping in the passenger seat and at his old Cadillac. He remembered that differently, too. He got out and walked to Sheila's door, opening it and pulling out her limp body, leaving Phil, Zach, and Kirsten to exit the vehicle by themselves.

Nice to be home, he thought as he turned on the television and walked to the couch, sitting as the picture appeared.

He carried Sheila to bed, wondering what was wrong with the situation he came home to and feeling lonelier than he could ever remember. She had been complaining about being nauseous and about the pain in her stomach since they left and had fallen asleep a short while before arriving. She would moan in pain every time he tried to engage Phil in conversation, making the ride silent.

He could feel the heat rise from her forehead as he placed his hand on it and put her to bed. She looked pretty sick and had shown no sign of wanting him around.

Phil was gone by the time he returned to the car to get Zach and Kirsten, and he couldn't remember seeing Phil's car as they pulled in. He had been calling his house all night but couldn't even get his parents to answer. Something was going on. He could feel it. He just didn't know what it was.

He stood and walked outside into the light of the full moon. He breathed deeply and looked over the parking area in front of him. His attention turned to the lone peak lit up by the full moon, and he thought he could see Roa-Ma running along the top of the ridge.

He missed them and would cherish the time he spent with them forever. He wondered if Ahm and Shree would ever get married and hoped he could help in some way. He walked inside, sat on the couch, and stared at the screen again. He kicked off his boots and stretched out, relaxing as a talk show host erupted from the screen.

The screams of Sheila emanated from their bedroom, waking him in a state of panic. He lifted himself from the couch and ran to the room before he knew where he was. He swung open the door and turned on the light. She lay on the bed with a cold sweat running off her brow and her back arching in time with each contraction that entered her body. He thought she was bleeding to death as he looked at the bloodied sheets, feeling shock and disorientation.

He ran to her side, grabbed her arm, and checked for a pulse. She moved as he ran his hand over her boiling head, going into shock.

"Sheila..." he whispered, waiting for a response. "Sheila." His voice rose, still not getting a response. "Sheila!" He yelled as he shook her body, trying to revive her. He ran to the living room, picked up the phone, and realized he didn't know any phone numbers or who to call. He ran cold water onto a towel under the faucet and returned to the room, placing it on her forehead.

He lay his head on her chest, hearing a faint beat and detecting her shallow breath. He wrapped her in the blankets she lay on top of and lifted her. *Oh my God*, he thought as panic overtook him, and he started running through the house and out the front door. He ran to his car, placed her in the back of the old Cadillac, and stood up, looking for the keys in his pocket.

He sprinted to the trailer to grab the keys and thought about Zach and Kirsten sleeping in their room. He grabbed the keys from the table, ran to their room, and wrapped them up in the blankets, covering them. He carried them to the car, gently placing them in the front seat. He jumped in the driver's seat, pumped the gas pedal, and fired the engine. Tears ran down his face as he rammed the car into gear, speeding towards the closest hospital he knew.

III-V

Roa-Ma leaned against the smooth rock chair one of his ancestors carved near the entrance of his home and stared into the stars. Hunting season was getting ready to start again, and it was time to return to work. He thought of the things he would have to put in order before starting and of the man from whom he had learned so much.

All in all, he succeeded in his attempt. Unfortunately, it wasn't the outcome he hoped for. When he first entered the communion the night of Sah's ritual, it was like nothing he had ever seen. The voices came from everywhere, and the noise from their cities was too much for him to take.

The feelings he felt were unlike those of his species and left him tight, tense, and angry. It was hard for him to stay there long, and he felt aged every time he came out. It scared him to see what they had become and what the end result of his species would be. He had to figure out how to save his species and knew he had the rest of his life to see if navigating this communion of lives and thoughts was possible.

He wondered what the consequences of entering their world would be and prayed they would give him the answers he so desperately sought. He looked at the scars on his chest and thought of his wife running through the forest and of his children when they were young. Regardless of the results, he knew he was about to find out.

He hadn't been able to get very far in his frequent trips, but from what he could see, it didn't leave his race much time. Their race added more population to it every day than they had in their entire species. The planet couldn't sustain them forever. He wondered how much time was left. It could be any time. From today to a couple of hundred years before, the scriptures of old would come to pass, but they would come to pass, and it would be too soon for them.

And where would they be without the trees and the animals they hid? What would happen when the heavens became polluted, destroying everything they knew? How would they defend themselves when the last hunt occurred? He thought as he breathed. A star fell from the sky, and another followed in the distance. He smiled, knowing he would do everything possible to stop it and that his children would live the best life he could give them.

It was the violence they possessed that came out during his sessions with the man, and that's what he was most concerned with. Individually, they were weak. Together, they were a force stronger than the strongest armies they could amass. They were all afraid, living their silent lives among one another, never knowing who they were or what they could possess together. They were filled with the rage and destruction that would one day destroy his kind and all that ever was. He hoped they would remain where they were for years to come, or that Mother Nature could figure out a way to stop them, or at least slow them down. He laughed. With their weak, pink, soft bodies, it should be easy.

But still, communing with them was very confusing. He needed more time to figure it out. During the first communion, he wondered if they had given the man too much of the potion and was happy it didn't kill him. He wondered if he did the right thing by sending him back.

He had grown fond of him and knew his family and small children would be happy to see him when he returned. Through the communion interaction, he knew there were too many of them. They all had outlandish stories, and no one would listen to him or his stories, and everything he tried to accomplish would silently go away. It wouldn't be long before he knew what reaction his actions would have.

He thought of his wife again and wished she would come home. He missed her so much. He looked at his chest and rolled his shoulder, looking at his back. He had healed, although the meat he lost caused an indentation in his back, and he knew hair would never grow on the giant scar covering it. He pushed on it, still feeling pain as his finger indented the skin. He had never told his children of the severity of his injury. Even now, he didn't want them to know.

He lost some movement in his arm and was sure the feeling would never return to his fingers or forearm. It had been hard doing his chores with his limited movement, and sometimes, it still hurt when he ran. The worst was that he couldn't judge hot, cold, or pain like he used to. After a few incidents of him burning and cutting himself, he was learning to compensate for the loss. He was amazed he could hide it from his children, but believed he had succeeded.

The memory of the gun blast would never grow dim. It hurt every time it replayed in his mind, and he wondered if this would be the thing to force him to finally step down from the council. His body wasn't reacting the way it once did, and his age would continue the degenerative process. He hated his body growing old while his mind stayed young, and was willing to push the boundaries.

He persuaded the council to approve his territory, the last large piece of ground since the beginning, to be split in half. Ahm and Shree would take over one-half of the territory and its associated duties. At the same time, he and Sah would maintain this half until something happened to him or Sah got married. None of which he could see happening soon.

Shree's house was only a half-day's run for him, and he planned to visit often. He missed her and the way she took care of him and the cave. With his being the last of the large areas left, it was the perfect solution.

He didn't know why he hadn't thought of it before. It would cut down Sah's duties and allow him and Ahm to attend the council meetings together. They could work together and watch out for each other, stopping them from making the same mistakes he had. Hopefully, it would keep them all alive.

Ahm was one of three brothers. Roa-Ma approved his parents' request to have another baby, hoping they would have a daughter after the two boys were born. There had always been a limit of two children per family, and the council strongly opposed him. There was a sudden influx of male children, and he knew they could use another female within their species. He overruled the council and approved it anyway.

Ahm was a disappointment to his family since the day he was born. Although he wasn't treated as an outcast, he was raised without supervision or training and wandered the lands since he was old enough to walk. Being the third male child in the family gave him no life and no hope of having a wife or territory of his own.

His supervision had been minimal throughout his life. At the same time, his older brothers were groomed to take over when his father died. He was left to care for himself and learned most of the ways independently. He wandered on to Roa-Ma's territory, meeting Shree a few years ago, and had been coming back ever since.

Ahm's life changed after meeting Shree, and his wandering slowed. He started helping his father and family even though he wasn't wanted. Roa-Ma always felt guilty for the boy's existence and had secretly taken him in, teaching him the ways of old. Roa-Ma was sure Shree and Sah never knew, and now he could gloat that this was his plan all along.

Before Ahm met Shree, Roa-Ma chastised him in front of the council for going near the cities of men. Ahm said he needed to know if there was a way to get around within them, and he was sure there wasn't. According to his story, he was never in any danger and got close enough to see some of their homes.

He never denied going, and Roa-Ma admired his honesty and curiosity. That was why he picked him to take the man back. Ahm learned quickly and possessed the integrity necessary to make him a great leader. Knowing that he would be attending the meetings every year with Sah and that he wouldn't have to make the trip much longer put him at ease, and he was glad he made the choice he had. Ahm would be able to help show Sah the way.

A flock of geese flew in formation and honked from above, setting the forest alive with the sounds and movement of all the creatures residing inside of it. Roa-Ma stood and walked to the cave, wandering around with nervous, bored energy. He sat beside the table, fidgeting, and looked for something to do. He wondered if his wife acted the same way Shree had when she learned the news of their territory opening.

He and his wife, Shar, waited a long time, courting and spending as much time together as they could while his father aged and died. His mother went soon after his father, and they were finally together. It seemed like a lifetime of him taking care of the territory and wanting her while he came home to his parents' slow demise. He

234

knew the feeling of wanting and wished they could have been married earlier, and he could have had more time with her.

He missed her and wished she could be with him, watching their children become adults. He knew she would like Ahm and would love where Shree was moving. They would escape to the same place when they wanted to be alone, so many years ago. To him, it was the most beautiful place on the planet. He hoped Shree was happy, and Ahm would easily fall into the role of being her husband.

It would be easy for him to run to their home at any time. He could ensure they were Okay and watch as his grandchildren grew up. He would have many long talks with Ahm, making sure his family came before his sense of adventure and curiosity. Sah, of course, would always remain the heir to the head of the council.

He wondered how much longer it would be before he joined his wife. He had abused his body throughout the years, and he wasn't sure how his body would handle the shock of the new communion. He was pleased that everything went so well. He knew he could safely transfer the memories of the man to Sah and Ahm, as well as his memories of past communions. He could also pass his interpretations of those memories when the time to join his wife neared. He stood, walking towards the wall, and exhaled as he reached it.

His thoughts returned to the man. He missed him and wondered how he and his family were doing and if he had found them. He still prayed for the day they could receive assistance from man and live together in peace and harmony. He knew now wasn't the time, and he wondered if Ahm and Sah would interpret the things he gave them differently than he did.

The pictures painted in his mind were too unbelievable for any of his associates to believe, and they turned their heads at the first sign of it. The speed of their life and the emotional turmoil they were experiencing every day left him a little weak-kneed and unbelieving himself.

He hoped that with enough time, the three of them could figure out what it all meant. Maybe they could be the ones to bridge this gap and bring the death and destruction to an end. Then, they could live in the open without the fear they now possessed.

He had the opportunity to look into a man's soul and live his life's dream. On his last communion, he heard a small voice beginning to flow into a branch of the humans. They were becoming as concerned with their world as the Keepers were with theirs. They were beginning to realize that their world was fragile and that their way of living was slowly destroying it. There was still a glimmer of hope.

He wondered if there was a way to make that voice grow as he stretched his back and walked from the cave. If things went as he thought, it could be his great-grandson dealing with the end. He had done what he could by opening up the territory for Ahm and Shree and allowing his son to become a man. He would make sure his family was happy for whatever time they had left.

He sat back in his chair, closed his eyes, and drifted to what it would be like when John's race and his collided. Man would outnumber them. They would quickly be overrun. The battles would be ferocious. He was almost sorry he wouldn't be alive to be a part of it. It would be nice to die for something.

He fantasized about fighting the battle himself and saw a man in the distance pull out a gun. He popped back to reality and stared into the sky. They would never survive.

In a way, he was disappointed in the species of man. He had expected a warrior, a destroyer, a savage beast. Instead, he got John. He laughed, being happy with what he found.

He leaned back and sighed as the music rang through the forest like the sounds of so many beautiful nights he spent in this wonderful world. He had done what he could and felt he had lived an honorable life. And after all, wasn't that really what life was all bout? He stood and walked to the cave's opening, staring out into the distance as Ahm and Shree appeared in the clearing below.

III-VI

John sat on the couch and sighed. He felt lightheaded and jittery as the smoke from his cigarette exited his mouth. He looked at it, hating what it was doing to his lungs, and took another drag.

During his time in the forest, he hadn't missed smoking. It didn't even seem to cross his mind. He had sworn he would never smoke again after Shree slapped the lighter out of his hand. But, as soon as he was home, the withdrawals started. Sheila was admitted to the hospital, and he heard the news of a baby for the first time. The betrayal was more than he could handle, and he bought a pack at the first convenience store he saw. He had been smoking a pack a day since.

He stuck the still-burning butt into an empty beer bottle and thought about his time in the forest. He had felt so healthy and had been running every day. He had never felt so strong and energetic. Now, his lungs hurt every morning, and he felt soft once again.

It had been almost a year since he returned home, and the sound of the doctor's voice still echoed in his head from that night. "I'm sorry," he could hear him say. "We couldn't save the baby, and we almost lost her." He stood stunned, unable to speak, as the doctor waited for a response and then walked away. He had been bewildered since.

Sheila refused to see him and decided rehab was the best place for her. *Maybe she was right*, he thought. He still hadn't been able to talk to her, and he hoped that after she sobered up, she would want to see him and the kids. They missed her terribly, and he wondered if they missed him the same way during his absence.

He knew who the father was; he just couldn't prove it, and no one in town wanted to discuss it. He found out about Phil's legal trouble when the D.A. came to his door, asking him questions about his contractor's license. The rest made sense. He wondered why he hadn't seen him around town and if he got through the charges he was facing, or if he was sitting in a jail cell.

He didn't hate him or Sheila for what happened, and wanted them to know that. He missed his wife and wanted so much to speak to her. He wished he were in the forest with the creatures who knew what family and friendship were. He never felt the loneliness with them that he did now.

Phil's parents called him and offered to buy his business. They were following their attorney's advice and were sorry for all Phil had done to him and his life. He knew what they were doing, and he really didn't care. He wasn't planning on doing anything to hurt him anyway, so he took the money.

It wasn't much, but Phil's parents came by with a cashier's check. They never talked about Phil while they sat before him, signing the papers, and he didn't have the heart to bring him up. He told them he hoped Phil was okay as they left, but it fell on deaf ears. He paid off some bills, bought a couple of keyboards, and a P.A. system with the money he received. Then he went to work for one of the largest construction companies in the county.

Zach told him that Phil had been there a lot and sometimes asked about Phil when he would ask about his mother. Neither of the kids ever mentioned Phil and Sheila hugging or kissing, and they were pretty closed up about the whole subject. He felt bad for them and all they had been through, so he never mentioned the subject.

He would always wonder what happened, what kind of relationship they were in, and if it was just a drunken night. He wasn't sure he wanted to know. Snapshots of Sheila flipped through his head as a knock sounded at the door. He turned his head toward it and slowly got up, opening it. An older lady in her mid-to-late seventies stood in the dim light, smiling.

"Hello, Mr. Smith, am I too early?"

"Hi, Mrs. Prescott; no, you're right on time as always." He smiled, "Come on in." She walked into the living room and looked at the house, figuring out what she would do while he was away.

"I put the kids to bed early tonight, and there's some munchies and food in the fridge in case you get hungry." He smiled his faint and depressed smile again and walked to the closet, pulling out his coat. "I gotta go now. We have to tear down tonight, so I won't be back until about the time you're getting up. I'll leave your money on the table when I get home. Okay?" She nodded as he slipped his arms through his coat and walked towards the door. He grabbed his keys from the table. "I gave you the number for the club in case you need me for anything, right?"

She nodded her head again and smiled. "Yes, Mr. Pierce, I have everything I need. Now you go and have fun. I'll make sure the children eat before I leave so you can get some rest."

He thought about how lucky he was to have found this lady. Her husband of forty years was a musician, and she supported him his entire life. John took his children to church one Sunday and met her as they were leaving. She heard of his band and thought she recognized him from the small-town newspaper.

The children loved her, and she offered her phone number to babysit, so he took it. She lived alone and had no family, so she enjoyed spending the night and getting up with the kids. He thought of his mother and wished she were still alive. The day of her death flashed into his mind, and a lump formed in his throat. He missed her so much. She was always the most important woman in his life, and he wished she were still alive, so he could share all that had happened with her.

A small bird sitting on a tree branch chirped as he walked out the door and onto the small porch. He pulled up the collar on his coat and looked up at the silvery moon, spotting the bird speaking to him. He hesitated, looking at the bird's beak. It was open and pointed to the sky, looking like the dead babies he had seen with Shree at the strip-mining site.

He did some detective work and discovered that the mining operation had ceased due to financial difficulties within the company. He started a petition against any further mining or the use of cyanide, bringing it to the communities' attention and pushing it onto a ballot, allowing the people to vote. Now, no other mining company would be allowed in the area, and the precious minerals would stay where they were forever.

The land would be turned into a bird sanctuary, and the extinction of the protected species that lived there would be stopped. A small victory, but a victory nonetheless. He would follow up periodically to be sure it remained that way, and he looked for anything else he could do.

He chirped, trying to mimic the bird, and laughed at his lame attempt. The bird tilted its head and looked down at him as he extended his finger. It took flight and veered down, landing on it. The trees came alive with the music he had finally figured out to use. *I'm trying,* John thought as he patted the bird's head. *Someday, we'll make this a better place for all of us to live.*

The bird looked at him and chirped, extending its wings and flapping from his hand. He watched through the bird's eyes as he flew off, disappearing into the night, knowing it was headed for Shree.

She had been right; he had been given a gift, and it had gotten easier as time passed. He had learned to enter Roa-Ma's world through the animals and was trying to teach it to his kids. He was always so calm while he was there, and the loving emotions he felt inspired him.

When he was there, he felt as though he could live forever and could sense Roa-Ma and his family. Sometimes, he could even talk to them. He finally understood what Shree was talking about when she said, "All of us." He felt calm, knowing they were all part of the same whole. With his new knowledge, he would be forever changed.

John parked his truck and opened the door. When he returned from the forest, he tried to explain what had happened to him. But after he noticed the looks he was getting from the officers interviewing him, he decided it would be better to tell them he was lost, survived by finding a cave for shelter, and ate bugs or anything else he could find. He wasn't sure they believed him, considering he was fully nourished and healthy, but it was better than being locked up in a loony bin. He also knew it would keep Roa-Ma and his family safe.

He stepped from his truck and walked into a small, smoke-filled room across the street. "Hey, Harry, can I get a Seven Up, please?" he asked as he walked by the bar. He looked at his watch. It was 8:45. Still plenty of time. He walked to a table and sat down, staring at the band's equipment. He pulled a cigarette from his top pocket, put it in his mouth, and lit it.

The waitress set the glass in front of him. "Here you go, John." She smiled as he picked it up and took a drink. He gave her a dollar for her troubles, and she walked away. He wished Sheila were here. He missed her company and knew the kids didn't understand what was going on.

Zach still believed his mom was away, just as he had been, and that she would be coming home soon. He hoped that was right, but doubted it. Kirsten was still too young to realize what was happening, and he wondered what went on in her mind. He knew they would be scarred for life, and he felt guilt for being taken from them.

He rolled the glass onto his fingertips and drank the rest of the cold liquid, swallowing hard and chewing on the remaining ice. He looked around at the few people in the bar and thought about his friends Roa-Ma, Shree, Sah, and Ahm. He was happy they were well. Shree and Ahm were happily married, and he heard she was pregnant with their first child. It still felt like a dream; sometimes, he would think he was waking up. If it wasn't for the animals that came around and his ability to understand them, he wouldn't believe it happened at all.

He looked at his watch. It was almost nine. *Where are they?* He thought as a small man with glasses stumbled up from behind him. "Hey, I know you, man," he slurred, spewing the smell of alcohol from his mouth. "Why don't you let me buy you a drink, buddy?" He put his hand on his back and laughed.

"Good evening, ladies and gentlemen." John could hear the singer say through his P.A. system.

"Thanks anyway, but I've really got to get to work right now." John slapped the man on the back, looking at the stage. *Work,* he thought, smiling as he walked towards it. *I pay the babysitter more than I make in a night.* He jumped onto the stage, hiding behind his keyboards and looking at his bandmates.

They didn't get to play out much, but it was what he knew he needed to do. They practiced a couple of times a week, and he wasn't spending the time with his children he wished he could, but he had something to say and wanted it heard.

After all the years of his music being pent up inside of him, his songs flowed like the rivers that would rush before him during his time in the forest. Perhaps someday he could do more, but for now, this would have to suffice.

He looked at the drummer as he counted. "One... Two... One, two, three, four!" John's fingers hit the keys simultaneously with the guitar, bass, and bass drum. His head cleared of everything but the music as it flowed through the small club like the chimes through the trees in the forest of his mind.

www.ingramcontent.com/pod-product-compliance
Lightning Source LLC
Chambersburg PA
CBHW022313280626
47169CB00020BB/2921